2011
Colonnade Writer's Anthology

Edited by Chris Murphy & Dealva Dowd-Hinkle

CJM Books
Rochester, NY

Contents & Rankings

Introduction

The Colonnade Writing Contest is an annual contest, judged in quarterly rounds, and followed up with an internationally distributed anthology of its winning entries. Last year, 2011, was the contest's first year, so I wanted to take a page or two to share with the reader all there is to know about the contest's inception, its corollary anthology, and the future of Colonnade.

Let me first congratulate all of the winning authors for their commitment to quality writing, their ability to stand out from a diverse pack, and of course their captivating short stories. It goes without saying that I've read all of the stories included herein, but it is a different thing to honestly say that I've enjoyed doing so. For that reason, I took it upon myself to go back and read all the other entries, and I only wish we could give away more prizes. In fact, as the anthology editor and contest administrator, I've found that to be the best part of my job, telling people they've won. Now I know why Ed McMahon did what he did. Thank you to all those who entered in 2011, and congratulations again to those who won.

My good friend, Kate Riley, and I often talk about book publishing, given our similar backgrounds as writers and coaches. Because of our current responsibilities as mentors and decision makers, these conversations often last for hours and weigh quite heavily on our minds. During one of these conversations, in the Spring of 2011, she reminded me of how she had always wanted to produce an anthology of works by some of the women in her writing groups and workshops. It was during this conversation that I proposed we create a contest out of it.

Because of her commitments at the time, Kate couldn't do too much with it, and instead encouraged me to move forward with it to see what could happen. A "don't-know-until-you-try" response from Kate Riley was typical, and I'm she would have told me I was crazy if she thought it was a bad idea. So, I went with it.

We started behind from the get-go, announcing the contest April 1st, missing a whole quarter's worth of entrees and winners and subsequently making this anthology about 25 percent smaller in page count. For that reason, you'll see there are only three parts to this anthology, not four, which *quarterly* implies.

Before long, the second quarter was over and we had over forty entries. I immediately called Kate Riley to share the good news. I think it was after the third quarter that she finally expressed enthusiasm for the contest and an interest in joining with CJM Books and myself, to make 2012 bigger and better.

So it is with great excitement that I am pleased to announce Kate Riley's alliance with the Colonnade Writing Contest. "Wait, what does that mean?" you ask. Simply put, the Colonnade Writing Contest has already added a non-fiction category, administered by Kate Riley, essentially doubling the contest's reach and scope of entries, just about doubling the size of next year's anthology, and more than doubling the amount in prize money awarded to its winners.

I almost forgot. One of the stories in this anthology has been awarded the grand prize of *Story of the Year* and a 500 USD cash prize. I don't want to spoil the fun, though, so if you haven't already heard about it online, just keep reading and look for the *Story of the Year* blowout (like the one on the cover) on that story's first page.

One of a Million Things

by Michael Gunter

On any given day, any one of a million things could change your life forever – a chance encounter, an unexpected phone call, a newspaper ad, a lottery ticket purchased on a whim. Most of these opportunities pass you by like buses in a city, carrying all the "someone elses" to their appointments with destiny. But then comes the day when the bus stops for you.

This is the story of one of those days.

It happened one cold morning in November. Anthony Robinson, a thirty-two year veteran of the Bay Area transit system, made his usual stop at the Quick Mart next to the bus station to warm-up his insides before boarding his cold bus. The bell on the door alerted the clerk, who was restocking the cigarette display above the cash register.

"Morning, boss," he called out as Anthony shook off the cold. "Heavy fuel be ready in a jif. How 'bout a muffin? Hot out the oven and good for gittin' rid of that ol' grumbly." He held out a plate of steaming blueberry muffins.

"Thank ya, Ty," Anthony replied. "Don't mind if I do." He took a muffin and tasted it. "Ooowee, your wife sho'nuff knows how to cook 'em up right. You a lucky man."

"I knows it, and you knows it, but let's keep Katie thinkin' she be the lucky one." Tyrone winked and the two men smiled that knowing smile. "Hey, Anthony, where you taken that magic bus of yours today?"

"Oh, I thought I'd go down to Florida," Anthony said, still smiling. "Maybe get me a little place on a beach somewhere. The way I figure, it'd take a good three, maybe four weeks to thaw out these old bones."

"I know whatcha mean. I'd love to get back to the South. Say, how's 'bout you take me with ya?"

"I'd do it if I could. I'd do it if I could. But until then, I'll be doin' my job like everybody else."

Tyrone chuckled. "You got the patience of Job, my friend. I don't think I could stand totin' those tourist all over the place all day long. Some o' dem folks give me the willies."

Anthony just smiled. "Ah, they ain't so bad. Just gotta think of 'em as little children. Besides, my regulars make the day worth getting' up for. They descent folk doin' what they got to do to get by. If I can be a part of that, I feel like I'm doing my good thing."

At the sound of the coffee pot timer, Tyrone filled a Styrofoam cup with the steaming black stuff.

"Say, Tyrone," Anthony said, nodding toward the lottery ticket display on the counter. "You suppose anybody really wins these things? I mean, you hear about 'em from time to time, but ain't never anybody I know. You ever know somebody to hit it big like that?"

"No, can't say as I do."

"What would you do with all that money?"

Tyrone thought for a moment as if he were being interviewed by Ed McMahon himself. "I'd get me a piece of paper and make a big 'Help Wanted' sign for that window over there and never look back. Then I'd go home and get Katie and get out of town to someplace warm and sunny. Shoot, we wouldn't even pack. Just buy everything new when we get there."

"Tyrone," Anthony said, "you must be the best salesman in the world."

"How's that?"

"I'll take one of them tickets."

"One lucky ticket for the man who drives the bus." Tyrone rang up the coffee and ticket and handed them both to Anthony. "And good luck to ya."

"Thank you," Anthony replied. "Oh, I almost forgot. How 'bout one of them napkins there?"

Tyrone put on a serious face. "It gonna cost ya."

Anthony played along. "All right, sir. How much?"

"Ah, shoot. I give it to ya."

The two men shared a laugh.

"Thank you, Tyrone. You're a good man."

"You're right for sayin' so."

Anthony stuffed his lottery ticket into his coat pocket and turned to leave. "Have a blessed day."

"You do the same."

The bus was cold, but started instantly, as if it knew who had turned the key. Anthony took a sip of his coffee and placed the cup on the dash, causing a small spot of fog to form on the glass just above it. He performed the routine check of gauges, lights, mirrors, and the onboard intercom system. Confident that all was in order, he took his cup and joined the other drivers in the terminal. Anthony liked this part of the day before they all went their separate ways. The idle chatter of so many working class philosophers was entertaining, and more times than not, he found himself pondering their musings throughout the day.

"Hey, Anthony," a middle-aged round man called out. "How's the gravy train?" Anthony's tenure had earned him the Golden Gate route in one of the more pleasant areas of San Francisco. Still, it had its own challenges, and Leon knew it, but liked to tease Anthony all the same. In actuality, Leon's own Sausalito route was even better and everybody knew it. Anthony raised his cup of coffee in Leon's direction and smiled. Leon seemed satisfied with the gesture and returned to the tall tale he was sharing with three other drivers.

Anthony found an empty chair next to young Jimmy O'Dell. Jimmy had been with the company for a little over a year. Some of the old timers gave the rookie a hard time, but most simply ignored him. Anthony took it upon himself to help Jimmy become a part of the team.

"Good morning, Jimmy," Anthony said as he took the seat. "Gettin' ready for the holidays?"

"Not much gettin' ready at my house," Jimmy replied. "Money's tight again this year."

"Oh, I heard that. Seems folks is gettin' futha and futha behind that ol' devil eight ball all the time. Now I got no head for business or the economy, but it seems to me a fella that works hard oughts to be able to make it just fine in this ol' world."

"It sure seems that way, Anthony."

"Well, don't you worry none. The good Lord gonna take care of His children. Besides, that's what Christmas is really all about, ain't it?"

"Yeah, I guess you're right." Jimmy stood up and put on his gloves. "Looks like it's time to roll."

"Yes, indeedy," Anthony agreed. "Time to get those people where they got to be. You have a nice day now, ya hear?"

"Yeah, you too, Anthony."

The two men joined the other drivers as they made their way to their respective buses. For the next ten minutes, the terminal parking lot resembled an aircraft carrier launching a squadron of planes. One by one, they rolled out onto the busy Bay Area streets.

Anthony's morning proceeded exactly as he expected. He made his three stops on the Oakland side of the bay, picked up his regulars, and entered the on-ramp to the Bay Bridge. He hummed a little tune and seemed genuinely happy to be right where he was. None of his passengers shared his enthusiasm. Some passed the time reading, checking email, and sending texts, while others tried to squeeze a few more minutes of sleep out of the morning. But most stared blankly out of the windows at the city, much of which was still asleep in the pale dawn of the new day.

As his bus approached the first stop on the San Francisco side, Anthony noticed a large group of tourists waiting for him. He correctly surmised that they were together as they all wore the same color jackets and each one sported one of those goofy looking stocking hats with the multi-colored plumes sticking straight up out of the top.

Anthony tried to guess what kind of group they were. Church group? Traveling school choir? Senior citizens touring club? Future Farmers of America? By the time he got close enough to see faces, it became obvious who they were – high school kids from the east coast on fall break. Usually these groups consisted of wealthy kids from the New England states sent on cross country "educational" tours. Typically, they were loaded with cash, but empty of manners.

When Anthony's passengers realized that the group would be invading their bus, they offered a collective groan from behind him. He pulled up to the stop, but had to wait to open the door. The mob pushed itself against the bus as if it were a single organism.

"Keep going!" someone shouted from the back of the bus.

Anthony simply flashed an understanding wave and waited for the group's leaders to gain control of the situation outside. Finally, Anthony opened the door, and a stream of shivering young people flooded the bus. They filled every vacant seat, assaulting those who were already on the bus with free-swinging cameras and backpacks as they made their way down the aisle. Once the group had settled into their seats, the first of Anthony's regulars pushed their way toward freedom at the front of the bus. As they exited, they eyed Anthony and smiled sympathetically as if they might never see him again. Anthony cheerfully returned their smiles and nods.

As the bus rolled back out onto the street, some of the group broke out into song while others in the group shouted for them to "shut up." Suddenly, a volley of balled up tourist maps erupted, and the bus looked like a food fight in a high school cafeteria. The group's leaders slunk down in their seats, hoping paper would be the extent of the barrage. The single mother in the seat directly behind Anthony looked more uncomfortable than usual, and the night club singer next to her just kept muttering things Anthony was glad he could not hear. They exited the bus at the next stop, along with the street vendor who told Anthony he would be praying for him. Anthony thanked him and continued on toward Pier 39 where he suspected and hoped he would leave the rowdy curmudgeons. Anthony was correct. As quickly as they came, the group disappeared into the throng already gathered at the Wharf.

The rest of the day was rather uneventful. Anthony completed his shift and returned to the terminal in Oakland. He clocked out, chatted for a few minutes with the shift supervisor, and made the short walk back home.

Anthony's apartment was small, but adequate for a single man. Its furnishings were modest and showed signs of age. Anthony bolted the door behind him and began his nightly routine. He emptied the contents of his pockets onto the kitchen table and hung his coat on the hook by the door. Next he pulled off his shoes, cracked the knuckles in his toes, and clicked on the television set on his way into the bedroom. There, he hung his uniform in the closet and pulled on a pair of worn sweatpants and an old T-shirt. He then went into the bathroom where he washed his hands and face. Looking at his reflection in the bathroom mirror, he was again surprised at the old man who stared back at him. For a man of sixty years, and hard years at that, he felt youthful. He often wondered if others saw him as he looked or as he felt. He hoped for the latter.

As he made his way back into the living room, he paused at the collection of photographs hanging on the wall. He gazed at each one, reliving the memories they held. On this particular evening, the first photograph took him back nearly ten years to his son's graduation from medical school. He was so proud as he watched him receive his diploma. Randy went on to become a very successful doctor in New York City. The next picture took him back even further. Anthony's daughter Chloe was the pride of his life. They used to go camping in the summers up at Lake Tahoe. He recalled the summer Chloe broke her arm while trying to climb a tree. He had held her all the way to the doctor, drying her tears with his shirt. Chloe grew up and married a lawyer who took her to live close to his parents in Atlanta. The last photograph was of his precious Claire. They had been high school sweethearts, marrying right after graduation. She was the most beautiful woman in all the world to him, and he never let a day go by without making sure she knew it. Cancer had taken her away from him five years earlier.

Claire's funeral was the last time he saw his two children together. Since then, there were occasional visits. But time and distance and the demands of life eventually turned visits into phone calls, and phone calls into cards at Christmas. It had been nearly a year since his last contact with either of his children. How he longed to go back in time, if only for one more moment – one more game of catch with Randy, one more hike with Chloe, one more slow dance with Claire. This part of Anthony's routine was often painful, but it was a pain he could not bare to let go. It was his connection with all that was good in his life. When he could stand it no longer, Anthony wiped his eyes and began preparing his evening meal.

The music at the beginning of the local news caught his attention. He turned to watch while the microwave oven put the finishing touches on his supper. Toward the end of the broadcast, the news anchor announced that the lucky numbers for the California Super Lotto would be announced after the commercial break. Lotto! Anthony had forgotten all about the ticket he purchased early that morning. He glanced over at the kitchen table and spotted it lying there with some loose change and an ATM receipt.

Now Anthony was not one to gamble. In fact, he often scoffed at people who put their hope in a system designed to take their money. Furthermore, he knew his chances of winning the lottery were about as slim as him becoming the first black man to go to the moon. It just would not happen. However, for some crazy, unexplainable reason, he had purchased the ticket. Anthony picked up the ticket and waited for the commercial break to end. At precisely 6:23 p.m., Anthony Robinson became a millionaire.

It took several days for the initial shock to wear off and the reality of it to set in. In fact, even as he deposited the initial installment of his winnings into his bank account, it really did not occur to him that he should be doing anything different as a result of his new financial status. Actually, he was kind of nervous about the whole thing. He had heard stories about lottery winners who's lives were literally ruined by it. If the wild spending sprees that exceeded their winnings did not do them in, it was the bitter jealousy of family and friends who felt they deserved a share. Anthony wanted to be smart about his good fortune, but he had no idea what to do or where to begin. So he simply stuck to his routine, told no one, and waited for something.

Five days after winning the lottery, Anthony's day off, he forced himself to begin thinking of what seventeen million dollars actually meant. It was an inconceivable amount of money to a sixty year old black man born and raised in the inner city projects of Oakland. Anthony had spent his entire life just getting by. The thought of extravagance was as foreign to him as his meager existence would have been to a Rockefeller. But there was something he had always wanted to do.

Anthony awoke early and took his time showering and getting dressed. As he wandered into his living room, he paused at the pictures on the wall and gazed at Claire's beautiful face.

"I wish you could be with me today, Sweetheart," he said aloud. "Oh, how I do wish you could be here today." He kissed his finger tips and touched them to the photograph.

After a leisurely cup of coffee and scan through the morning paper, Anthony donned his best coat and hat and greeted the new day. Down at the bus station, Anthony approached the ticket window. He smiled as Maria recognized him from behind the counter.

"Good morning, Anthony," she said cheerily. "Aren't you off today?"

"Yes indeed," Anthony replied. "I'm here as a payin' customer today."

Maria stared at him as if he had just spoken to her in a foreign language.

He continued. "I'd like one ticket to Sausalito, please."

"You wanna buy a ticket? Are you serious? You do know you can ride for free, don't you?"

"Oh, yes. I know the company handbook says I can ride for free, but I would like to buy a ticket."

Maria shook her head as she took Anthony's money. The thick glass prevented him from hearing her mutter, "One lousy perk from the company and he wants to buy a ticket? Must be too many hours behind that wheel." She slid the ticket through the pass-through tray and stared at Anthony.

"Thank you, Maria. I hope you have a real nice day."

"You, too, Anthony."

He got the same bewildered look from Leon as he boarded his bus and handed him the ticket. "Good morning, Leon. Extra hours, eh?" He had not expected to see Leon behind the wheel as they had the same days off.

"Yeah, holiday's a-comin'." He watched Anthony in his rearview mirror take a seat toward the rear of the bus.

Anthony had driven over the Bay Bridge so many times he could accurately judge the bus's location on the bridge based solely on the sound of the tires rolling over the seams and other inconsistencies in the road. Once on the other side he knew every building, every traffic signal, and every pothole from the base of the Bay Bridge to the Golden Gate. Yet even with such familiarity, he sensed an excitement about being there. There was just something about San Francisco he could never get over.

The ride over the Golden Gate bridge was less familiar to him, though he had been over it many times as well. As it faded in and out of the dense early morning fog, Anthony's excitement grew. He leaned forward in his seat and pressed his nose to the window as Sausalito came into view. The last time he had been in the small town was with Claire five years earlier. The last time they had been out together was in Sausalito.

Anthony spent the early part of the day strolling through the downtown shops. He ate a light lunch in a coffee shop overlooking the bay and caught a late afternoon movie. It was certainly not the display of extravagance one would expect from a lottery winner, but for Anthony, it was exactly what he wanted. He could not remember the last time he had spent an entire day simply living in the moment with no regard for time, cost, or expectations. He found himself wondering if this was how wealthy people lived all the time. With that, he finally sensed an excitement about his good fortune.

The sun was low in the sky when Anthony entered one of the restaurants on Point Bonita. This particular restaurant was situated at the end of a long pier so every table in the dining room had a view of the water. Anthony followed the maitre d' to a small table next to a large window. The maitre d' pulled out the chair for him and offered him a menu. Anthony knew the courtesy was his for a price. He could tell by the way the man sized him up and the stares he received from the other patrons that he was not exactly in league with the usual clientele. But this was not the first time his presence had been merely tolerated, and he refused to let it ruin his fine day.

Anthony noticed there were no prices listed on the menu so he started to look for what he thought would be the least expensive entrée, but then caught himself. Old habits are hard to break. He closed the menu, sat back, and began to enjoy the view of the fishing boats coming in for the night. A girl dressed in black and white set a glass of water on the table and informed Anthony that his waiter would be along in a few moments. She was correct. Before long a waiter approached his table and welcomed Anthony to The Point.

"Are you ready to order, sir?" the young man asked. He seemed much more sincere than the maitre d'.

"Yes, I would like the filet mignon and lobster tail."

"Excellent choice, sir." The waiter said. Then he hesitated for a moment and asked, "Would you care to know the price on that entrée?"

"No, thank you," Anthony replied. "Why do you ask?"

"I, uh, just thought that," the waiter was scrambling for a polite explanation. "Well, that is one of our more expensive selections, and I thought..."

"That's okay, young man," Anthony said, trying to head off further embarrassment for the waiter. "I'm prepared to pay whatever the cost."

"I do apologize, sir," the waiter said, regaining his composure. "How would you like your steak cooked?"

"Medium-well."

"And to drink?"

"I would like a glass of your house wine, please, with my meal."

"Very well, sir."

The waiter disappeared, and Anthony settled back in his chair, returning his gaze out toward the ocean. The sun had just touched the horizon, splashing a dazzling array of color onto the partly cloudy sky. Anthony could not remember a more beautiful sunset in all his life. He watched the display until the sun disappeared and the blackness from the east took possession of the sky. The running lights from the few remaining boats gave the illusion of a fluid city in slow, yet constant motion. Anthony lost track of time and was startled when the waiter returned with his meal. The steak was cooked to perfection, as was the lobster. Anthony could not remember a meal quite like it. Once again, he wondered if this was standard fare for the wealthy.

After his meal, Anthony paid the bill, left a generous tip which surprised the waiter, and stepped out into the night. The air was frigid, but Anthony felt warmed by the experiences of the day. He walked leisurely down the street until he came to an inn.

As he entered the lobby, the clerk behind the desk eyed him suspiciously. Anthony approached the man and asked for a room.

"I am terribly sorry, sir," the clerk said, "but we are booked up for the night. Perhaps you will find a room down the street at the Motel 6."

"I see," Anthony said, a hint of disappointment in his voice. Nonetheless, he maintained his good mood and turned to leave. Before reaching the door, he overheard a well dressed Caucasian couple ask if there were any vacancies.

"Of course," the clerk said without hesitation, failing to notice Anthony standing not ten feet away. "We have a room on the second floor facing the bay and several on the first floor facing the garden."

Anthony waited patiently while the couple decided on one of the first floor rooms. They paid the clerk and walked hand in hand past Anthony, oblivious to his presence. Anthony approached the desk again and waited for the clerk to finish entering data into his computer. After what seemed like an unnecessarily long time, the clerk finally looked up. "Can I help you, sir?"

Anthony calmly removed his hat and placed it on the desk. "I would like a room please. Preferably one on the second floor facing the ocean."

Realizing his bluff had been called, the clerk tried to play it off as if their first encounter had not occurred. "One moment, sir." He pretended to scan through the data base. Finally, he cleared his throat and said, "Yes, sir, we do have one room left. However, it is one of our suites, and because of the holiday season, the price on that unit has gone up. And we have a family coming in tomorrow morning, so you would need to check out by ten. I really do think you would be more comfortable in another..."

"I'll take the room." Anthony interrupted.

The clerk shifted and fidgeted nervously with his pen. "Of course, this room is a non-smoking room, so..."

"I don't smoke." Anthony began to sense emotions from his younger, more volatile days; emotions he thought had mellowed with the passage of years and the love of a good wife. He felt his eyes squint and the muscles in his jaw tighten. Then, as he spoke, he heard an uncharacteristic edge in his voice. "Sir, I don't mean you no disrespect. If you don't think I can pay the bill, let me ease your mind." Anthony laid three crisp one hundred dollar bills on the desk. "Go on, check 'em. They real. But if it's a fuss you worried about, let me ease your mind on that one, too. I'm a sixty year old man who's wantin' a nice sleep and that's all. Now if it's something else that's got you all uptight, you're gonna have to tell me, because I can't read your mind."

"Take it easy, sir. Just take it easy," the clerk said nervously. He was half Anthony's age and slightly larger, yet his conscience had been pricked and he was backing down. "I will need you to fill out this registration card and I will need to see your driver's license."

Anthony complied.

"That will be two hundred dollars," the clerk said, avoiding Anthony's gaze.

Anthony retrieved one of the three bills still laying on the desk and tucked it back into his wallet. As the clerk slid the room key across the desk, Anthony took hold of his hand before he could withdraw it. They clerk flinched, but Anthony held is hand firmly. His expression softened as he looked into the man's eyes. "Young man," he said, "I don't know why the good Lord made us the way He did, and there ain't nothin' we can do about that. But as different as people are, we all have the same needs. And that's somethin' we can do somethin' about. I hope you and your family have a truly blessed Thanksgiving." With that, Anthony took the key and left the clerk to ponder his words.

The night brought Anthony restful sleep and blissful dreams. He dreamed of his Claire and Randy and Chloe. The four of them were gathered around a camp fire, roasting marshmallows and talking about the little things in life most people think of as unimportant until those things are gone. When he awoke the next morning, he could not remember the details of the conversation, only that it was pleasurable. He lay awake for a long time without moving, just enjoying the memory. Then his thoughts began to drift into the present. He thought of the people with whom he interacted each day. He thought about Tyrone and his dream to take his Katie someplace warm and sunny. He thought about Jimmy and wondered how old his kids were. He thought about the people who rode his bus each day. He wondered if they had fond memories, or if they were creating the memories they would one day revisit in their old age.

Suddenly, Anthony experienced something he would later describe as a moment of clarity, like descending out of the fog that so often shrouds the Golden Gate bridge. He dressed quickly and almost jogged back to the bus stop where he caught the transport back to his world on the other side of the bay.

Over the next few weeks, the regulars on Anthony's bus found a much more talkative driver. Anthony made it a point to learn each of their names and find out something about them. As he listened to their stories, he began to notice a common thread running through each of them. These were real people, with real hopes and dreams. The only thing missing was an opportunity – a chance to get out from behind, as Anthony put it, "that ol' devil eight ball."

As Christmas approached, Anthony's Yule Tide cheer became contagious. One day, while singing a Christmas carol, Anthony noticed the passengers in the seat behind him singing along with him. Soon more passengers joined in until the entire bus was alive with song. Passengers who had been riding with each other for years, but had never spoken, wished each other holiday blessings. Even the tourists seemed a little less annoying. Suddenly, the commute, which was once a dull prelude to dreary day on the job, became an enjoyable encounter that some of the passengers believed made the rest of the day just a little more tolerable.

Finally, Christmas Eve came. It was a Tuesday. Anthony left for work with a bundle of cards tucked under his arm and a little extra skip in his step. He stopped by the Quick Mart for his usual cup of coffee. He chatted briefly with Tyrone, gave him a card, and headed on to the terminal. He saw Jimmy just as he was climbing onto his bus. He seemed downcast for having to work the holiday, but was happy to see his only friend. Anthony wished him a Merry Christmas and gave him a card. As each of Anthony's regular passengers boarded his bus, he greeted them and gave each one a card with their name neatly printed on the envelope. He asked them to put it in a safe place and not open it until they got to work. Anthony spent the rest of his day shuttling tourists and last minute shoppers around the Golden Gate district. He imagined the expressions on the faces of his friends as they opened their cards to find the $100,000 he placed in each one.

It was only a matter of weeks before Anthony said "goodbye" to his last regular passenger. He didn't see them again except for on the rare occasion when one of them would stop by just to ride the old route again and chat with the man who changed their life. He did receive postcards from time to time, mostly around the holidays. He cherished every note, but for each person who received the gift from Anthony, it was their first note that found its place tacked up on the wall next to the photographs of Claire, Randy, and Chloe.

Dear Mr. Robinson,
We closed today on our new home in the Oaks. It's a nice neighborhood, and little Tommy has seen some boys his age he is eager to meet. Classes start in a couple weeks at the University. With any luck, I will be able to complete my degree in two years. I hope to open

my own business. All this has been so exciting, but the thing I am most thankful for is that I get to eat breakfast and supper with Tommy everyday, and I am here when he gets home from school. Thank you again Anthony for making all this possible. You're an angel.

Love,
Linda Carson

Dear Anthony,
New York City is a crazy "little" town. I got here three months ago, found a small apartment, and got a gig in an uptown club. Not those smoke filled meat houses I used to play in San Fran, people here actually have manners. Anyway, after only a week, this big wig from Venture Records comes in and hears me sing. To make a long story short, I go into the studio tomorrow to start recording my first CD. After that, they are sending me on a six month tour to promote it. I'll call you when I get to California. I'd love for you to come see me. Thanks, Anthony, for making this happen. Look for your name on the liner notes.

Love ya,
Amanda Martin

My dear friend Anthony,
Many thanks again for all you have done for me and my family. My wife and children will arrive from Delhi tomorrow. I am so happy to show them their new home in America. Also, my brother and I are putting the final touches on our new store in Los Angeles. It is called Anthony's Magic Carpet. I am hoping it is okay to use your name. What you did for us was pure magic from a good heart.

Your friend,
Aji

Dear Anthony,
I didn't know if you read SF Gourmet magazine or not, so I have enclosed a copy – see page 23. My restaurant was voted "Best New Dinner House" in the city. Anyway, I would like to invite you to our celebration night next Friday. Of course, your dinner will be on the house. It's a long way from that old hot dog and pretzel cart. And I owe it all to you.

Yours truly,
Gordon Johnson

Dear Tony,
It has been six months since I painted my last portrait on the pier. I do not miss it, even a little. I was in Paris last month and painted

lovers on a bridge. Then I went to Germany and painted the castles. Next, I am on my way to England and Scandinavia before I return home to Italy where I will paint mama. She is ninety-nine years old and can hardly wait to see her baby boy. I just hope she no pincha the cheeks. Mama says Maria has been asking about me. Maybe this old man still has it, eh Tony? Thank you again, my friend, for helping me find my way home.

Gratsi,
Antonio de Lucci

Dear Anthony,

Just a quick note to let you know how your generous gift has changed our lives. Kathy and the kids and I moved back to Reno and found a nice house. Just in time, too. Little Anthony was born yesterday – 7 pounds, 6 ounces. He's a handsome son of a gun. I can't wait to tell him about the man whose name he shares. I only hope he grows up to have a heart like that man. Thank you, Anthony, for all you've done. If you are ever in Reno, give us a call. We'd love to see you.

Sincerely,
Jimmy O'Dell

Dear Anthony,

Katie still thinks she is the luckiest woman in the world. And you know somethin'? I'm beginnin' to believe she's right. Florida has been very good to us. You should see me – ten pounds lighter and lookin' good. I don't understand why you stay on the West Coast. Florida is where it's at. Seriously, though, I can't stop thankin' you for gettin' me out of Oakland. I miss you and wish you'd come on down to the fun and sun.

Your best friend,
Tyrone

The recipients of Anthony's generosity all honored his request that no one know the source of their "inheritance" as Anthony liked to call it. They quietly closed one chapter of their lives and excitedly began new ones. When asked why he did what he did, Anthony's reply was always the same: "I had a dream one night, and I believe the good Lord was tellin' me to invest in the future. So that's what I did."

Anthony still drives the Golden Gate route and he has a new group of regular passengers. He knows all their names and they know his. He knows what they do for a living and he knows the things they hope for and dream about. He also knows that on any given day, any one of a million things could change their lives forever.

About Michael Gunter:

"I started writing in 2001. My works include both fiction and non-fiction books, short-stories, and essays. I am currently working on my third novel."

Pushcarts & Highballs

by Benjamin R. Hostetter

This is your story, Garland Starkweather; a love letter to those still fighting.

* * *

You have been in an accident. The hospital band reads, Admitted: Saturday, 10:36PM—May 20th.

Your wife, Rinette, is crying. You can do nothing to stop this. She cries into the uniform cut from your body. It is bloodied and in ribbons. The uniform glitters under the blinding, white hospital light. The remains of your Oldsmobile windshield cling to its fabric. She does not seem to notice though. She does not wipe away the blood, nor does she wipe the streams of tears that come. She cries on, and you can do nothing.

You were driving—plowed your Oldsmobile into a damn sycamore tree.

* * *

A month has passed since the accident. Yesterday you were released. The hospital band has been cut and discarded, and your wrist shows a tan line.

Rinette has left you to rise. You have, and you sit in the wheelchair you were given. You are paralyzed from the waist down. You are stuck. Bedroom walls surround you, and you're alone.

The bed is made. Its sheets and comforter are white. The cloth is fine, Rinette says. You should be proud as a peacock, but peacocks are nothing you care for—not especially. The thread count is very good, she says. You should have a look. You did, and after, you were told to feel. You did and said you did not think much about it—about counting threads.

The bed is a blank canvas, not like the eggshell walls Rinette says brings balance to the room. Paintings do the same, she says. Paintings are all around. You do not understand the art she collects, or why she collects it. Brings light to the room, she says. You think differently, and your eyes close. You list all the sad painters brightening the room, those Rinette has named for you: Hopper, Pollock, and Van Gogh.

Your eyes open—slowly—and Room at Arles stares back. It hangs above the bedpost. It was the Dutchman who threw it together. The room he painted reflects yours. It reflects you. The perspective is shot to hell.

The bookcase is organized by subject: Art, Politics, Philosophy, and so on . . . the bedside lamp, the rocking chair in the corner, the picture of Rinette and you, which sits atop Wittgenstein and lost faith . . . everything, it is all much taller than before. You are small in your wheelchair. You reach for the picture but stop short.

The picture shows Rinette, and by her side, a young man. You recognize him but not so much. He stands tall—taller than you.

Rinette's graduation, you think. The day is windy, and Rinette's hair trails behind in streams of yellow. Above, an arch of red and white balloons beat about madly, as if applause is all around, and you smile. Rinette smiles. She has her diploma. She waves it. It reads: Master's in Fine Art and Art History. Her plans are to teach, she tells you. How wonderful, you say. She pinches your elbow. She tells you she will wait. She will be here when you return. She has caught wind of your deployment, but you say nothing in return. News of war is all over, but you say nothing. You push it aside, and you hug her—cup the small of her back—and touch your nose to hers. You are warm. Rinette and you beam—

You do not know the young man in the picture. He stands so tall, and he is happy. He smiles. You are not that person. The mirror says so. It reveals a man broken. That man is you. You are a fraction of what you used to be. Your hair is graying, and it is thinning. A beard shows. You want to shave it but cannot. The shaving kit sits too high on the bathroom sill. Nothing is in reach.

The mirror points out the obvious. Your clothes no longer fit. Atrophy is the word. Wasted away you call it. You're a damn pushcart, and in your lap a faded shoebox sits. It is something Rinette knows nothing about. You hide it from her.

Inside is the uniform you wore the night of your accident. It glitters still—red and white. You were asked whether you wanted it to be thrown out, and you said no. You took it and wrapped it in plastic. You tucked it away in the way back of the bedroom closet. You have tied a string to the bunch so to pull on it if needed. It is now you have pulled on it. Rinette does not know you have done this.

Under the bloodstained uniform is your old college jersey. There was a time you played football, but that was long ago. Star quarterback, all had said, but you never took stock in it. You push the uniform and jersey aside, and at the bottom a gun lies—loaded—all chambers full. You were issued it as an enlisted man. You were told to turn it in after the accident, but you have not. You were not questioned either, as if personnel knew you would need it.

You wrap your mouth around the barrel of the gun, and you think of Rinette when you do. The gun shakes. The bullets in the chamber rattle. Your hands were once steady, but now they tremble; and your teeth chatter, too. You bite down but wonder: Is wrapping your mouth around the business end of a gun anything like the screwing you once did but no longer can?—If you pull the trigger and the hammer slams, will you be but a splattered mess?—Will you stain the blank canvas that is the sheets Rinette recently washed?—Will you be but another sad painter brightening the room?

The taste is nothing you expected. It is shoe polish. It is talcum powder. It is the taste of wet cotton, which makes you shiver all over. You are cold. You are cold like the cold barrel of the gun. You did not expect to be so cold. You did not expect to think of some windy day—of a time when you were once warm. And spit gathers. It drips from the muzzle down your throat, and you swallow. Your eyes close once more. Do the right thing, you think.

Rinette calls from the kitchen.

"Garland, are you up and moving?"

Your wheels rock, and they squeak. You mouth, "Not for long," but the words have a hard time forming around the barrel of the gun. Your mouth waters, and the spit runs down your chin and on into your beard. You can do nothing about this, or the damn whiskers growing on your chin. The shaving kit sits too high.

"Garland?"

The chamber turns but does not click. The hammer moves in slow motion.

"Garland?"

The bedroom door opens.

You spit out the gun then hide it.

"What? What is it?"

"I was seeing if everything is all right—if you're fine. It's been a while."

You stammer, and she asks what it is you have. Nothing, you say. It's nothing but an old shoebox, really. "I'm only putting it away because there's no use for it now. Not any more." You lie to your wife.

"Have breakfast with me. Please. It's sad eating alone."

I will push you, Rinette says. She does, too, before you can tell her no. Before you can say don't.

* * *

Room in New York is framed above Rinette buttering toast. You hate it. It divides the kitchen in two. Hopper, you think. Damn him. He has painted a couple worlds apart. Though it is but a coffee table and doorframe separating the two, it might as well be all of the Atlantic. Rinette's back is to you, and the knife she has scratches. You reach for her, but she is too far. You stop short. You make a fist. Veins show. Your hand has gone white.

"Do we really need all these damn paintings?"

Rinette sets a second plate, and you ask why anyone in their right mind would ever want so many. "Is it necessary, really? What kind of person fills a room with a bunch of little paintings of fruit and flowers?"

They don't have to be little, she says. We can have ourselves some very big ones. "If that pleases you." Rinette fiddles with the toaster, which sits between the microwave oven and refrigerator. Her shirt rides up her back. Skin shows, and you realize she has kept her figure over the years. The same as the day you met.

Rinette is an active woman, you know. She does her exercises: yoga and ballet, and something she calls meditation. You do not understand it, but she seems to like it very much. It appears to work, as does her diet. She eats healthy: no red meat, plenty of fish, and the suggested amount of whole grains. She washes it all down with a combination of water and various fruit juices: cranberry, apple, and orange. And every so often she will have a glass of white wine, which is fine. A doctor will tell you the same, and she agrees. You recall a time her mentioning dragging from a Pall Mall filtered cigarette, but she did not like it so much. She had done away with it and said later, "It was the first and the last time," and "It's not that I want to live forever, but I do want to stick around for a while," and "I'm not done with you just yet." It was something the two of you had laughed about, but now you cannot help the thought if she had only let herself go this would be easier—and, damn it her shirt rides higher.

You want to touch her but you cannot. You're a damn pushcart, and you've been parked. You're alone at the table, left to look on from afar. Rinette turns the toaster on and off, and it clicks and it beeps.

The toaster isn't what it used to be. It burns Rinette's Wonder bread. Yours too. She will surely throw it out and replace it with a new toaster—a better toaster, one that shines—something that will do as it advertises.

"Why would anyone ever want a bunch of doodles hanging about the kitchen?"

You point to the cupboards, the sink, and the refrigerator, too. Rinette does not notice; her back is turned. You shift in what you now call a rolling prison, and you push up on its arms.

There had been no time to return the gun to its hiding place. You had slipped it beneath you. It presses up into you, and you are set off-balance. You sit crooked. "It doesn't make a lick of sense," you say. And the gun persists. "There's no point, really."

Rinette adjusts the toaster's settings then turns its dials. She fills it with two slices of white bread then stands on her toes. She looks down onto the glowing insides of the broken appliance.

"The point isn't where they hang but—what hangs." Rinette reaches for her buttering knife and sticks the toaster with it. The toaster sparks. "The way I see it. It's nice to have something that doesn't fade or go to waste. A painting is one way, and that's it. Not like feelings at all. They're not one thing one minute and another the next." She then pulls the knife from the toaster. Butter drips from its end. Drops fall to the ground.

You use the word symbolism because Rinette throws it around often. "You have the tendency to take something and paint it with a whole mess of symbolism."

"I do because it is."

Not at all . . . It is nothing more than a bunch of lines, shapes, and colors. "There's nothing more than that." You then pick a phrase she uses. "It's nothing more than an 'abstract impression.' It's nothing real, not really."

The toaster smokes. A black-gray cloud builds and builds. It masks Hopper's couple, suffocating them. Rinette has turned a heel. She leaves the blurred two to choke. She crosses the kitchen then sits opposite you. The smoke-cloud reaches the ceiling, then parts. It travels to each of the room's corners.

"I thought I told you to put Hume down, at least for the morning. It's not well of you to break apart the world so early."

You do not know what a Hume is. Do you find it at the local hardware store?—Is it between the nuts and bolts?—Is it something the farmers' market has to offer?—Is it a prescription the pharmacy down the way can fill?

"I'm not breaking anything," you say, "nothing that hasn't already broken."

Rinette lifts a hand then brings a finger to her mouth. Her mouth moves but nothing sounds. She pulls at her bottom lip then bites her fingernail. She is thinking, you know. She eyes the kitchen floor—all the tiling your wheels have scuffed. Rinette closes her eyes, and her forehead furrows. Without looking up she reaches for your hand. She takes it in hers. You pull back, but she holds tight. She says nothing. You say nothing.

You cannot help the thoughts coming. Like a loaf of bread, if you are to remain, you will soon mold—grow fur (more than you have already)—stink up the place—be thrown out. You can do nothing to stop this from happening. It is not in you, not any more. What is in you?—You sit. You roll. You scuff the kitchen floor. Rinette doesn't need her floor scuffed. What good are you?—You have nothing to offer your wife, not any more. What do you have to say?—What is left for you to say? And you realize: Silence. Rinette has quit singing; she hasn't sung since your accident. You damn the accident. You blame your legs. You miss your wife's sweet-sounding voice—the singing she once did.

And a melody comes; it beats about your head. You do not know why. It just does. It goes:

The man takes the car/ the car takes the man/ hi-ho, the Derry-o/ and she stands alone.

"Please say something. Garland, anything."

"I—"

* * *

You recall the day—a month, two months past. Rinette had asked whether the mail had come.

It has, you say. And you bring it to her. She's in the kitchen. You sit with her at the table. You pull up beside her. The perfume she wears reminds you spring has come.

"The University throws an Annual May Ball," she says.

You nod. How very nice for them, you say. You pet Rinette's leg. Fresh, she says then swats your hand. She unfolds the letter and reads down the page. We have been invited, she says.

"I am sure you will have a very nice time."

"We will have a very nice time."

You stand and go to the refrigerator. You stick your head in and count the apples.

"You cannot honestly say you can see me bopping about some ball. That sort of thing is no place for any roughneck." You count the oranges then the eggs. "It's not a place for the likes of me." You look up and over the refrigerator door. You lean on it, your arms hanging over its side—crossed. They sway a bit, to and fro. "Rinette, really. Look at me."

Your hands are calloused. Hair has started to grow from your nose and ears, knuckles, too, and your brow is thicker than it has ever been. "I'm a brute," you say.

"You're my brute," she says. "Anyway, I'm sending your mess uniform to be cleaned."

You cross the kitchen. Behind, the refrigerator door swings shut. You stand above where Rinette sits. She looks up from her seat. Her eyes say you'll do this because I have asked you to. And you rub her shoulders to say it's but a hard time you're giving her.

"Well," you say. "There seems to be no way around it."

* * *

You recall the night of your accident:—May 20th, hours before your collision.

The ballroom is gilded and full. It is rotating, and in the corner a pianist plays.

"What have you gotten me into?"

Rinette straightens your tie then picks lint from you lapel. She uses the word debonair.

"The sign out front is clear," you say. "No pets allowed."

"Then we're both in trouble." And Rinette winks, and she smiles, which says you're in it together. This comforts you; you don't know why.

Tenures and benefactors, who wear pressed and double-breasted suits, are all around—well oiled and shaven; their square chins jut and hover, as if defying gravity, sweet-smelling smoke spills out their mouths. Rings are made, punctuated by the men's puckered kisses, which follow each escaping puff. The men direct their stares, their mock kisses, pointing to the women they have brought, whose faces are painted redder than a Georgian summer night. You know this some how, as if in the back of your head the difference between a Georgian night and a Virginian—or some other—is clear and sharp. You convince yourself of this and go on then to take in the ballroom's decorations: sequins everywhere, shimmering and sparkling.

In the middle a chandelier hangs. Its blinding, white light washes over the bruised hardwood floor. It washes over all the men who have taken the hands of women who—after cigarettes are lit—are led onto the dance floor where, beneath the chandelier, they Waltz and they Jitterbug. The light shines down and makes them glitter. Glasses are held high, and cheers sound. How wonderful, you hear. Hi-ho, and all the pretty men and women praise the party for its glitz—its glam.

Smoke fills the ballroom, and conversations rise. Between step counting and cigarette lighting, there is talk of Van Gogh and of his yellows fading. His sunflowers are going to pieces. They are turning brown. You have nothing to add to the conversation, but think it sad all the same. So note: In clouds of smoke the sad, pretty faces glow, and they smile. For parties are to die for, you hear all around, from those men and women. They dance and they jig, and they bop, and their buckles and bracelets and cufflinks dazzle. All is bright and shiny beneath the chandelier. Everything sparkles; you do not trust it, really. And the piano plays on.

How very easy it is to be close at such great parties, Rinette says. It is a privacy not found in a coffee shop, or grocery store, or any place like that. To have a decent conversation, she tells you, the whole world has to have a ticket. Big, big parties are so very private, and Rinette waves to the crowd. The conversations have gone from dying flowers to endowments and John the Baptist. You see, she says, we can do whatever we want. There's not a person here who knows we exist. Big, big parties are so very wonderful. Let's take our clothes off and wave our underpants round and round, and we'll have ourselves a song; we'll sing—say—One Life to Live. For not a head will turn. We're our own private island, you and I.

"You see," she says. "It's a world well lost."

The pianist breaks and champagne is passed from hand to jewel-studded hand. You're asked if you would care for a glass and you wave the server off. The water you have is just fine, you say. It's all you need, really, but maybe Rinette would care for some. She, too, waves him off and says the atmosphere is filling enough. The server nods then offers a cigarette—to light it, too. And Rinette declines. "I'm no chimney," she says. The server bows and says very well. His hands are as calloused as yours, and you wish he had not bowed—asked if the two of you cared for any champagne, a cigarette. You try to hide the fact you are blushing. And it is then you realize, because of Rinette you attend such functions put on by the University. You're there for her, not because of any elbow rubbing you hope to do. You're supportive.

Rinette admires the hanging chandelier. Opulent is the word she uses. She is a smart woman; she knows very big words. And you say yes, and "It must be a fake." To which Rinette laughs.

The pianist sees his cummerbund has shifted. He pulls it down then buttons his jacket. He sits and settles himself. He sighs then strikes the black and white keys, and the music plays on.

"What a lovely party," Rinette says.

Lean in, you say. And Rinette does. The warmth of her breath breaks across your face. A loose strand of hair has fallen over her eyes, and you pick at it. You push it behind her ear where you then whisper. You hope to speak softly. She will think it endearing. And though you try, it is not what you want. It is rough. It is hard—deep with a rasp, which kills you.

Escape with me, you say. Come out from under the chandelier, and you say opulent. "Run away with me."

Rinette's hand reaches. It brushes past your cheek. You let it. She pets the back of your neck. It's not so rough, she says, and you don't know why, but you like this. She kisses you. Her lips are soft and wet. And you try not to think about screwing, but you do anyway—of tearing back the sheets the two of you share, of letting her and your clothes fall to the floor—And Rinette pulls you closer. There is a place, she says. And she points. It is just beyond a group smoking and drinking and clinking the glasses they have, and the dresses they wear, which shimmer, touch the floor and sweep at spilt ash.

There's a painting there, Rinette says. I want to show you it. She reads your mind, you say, though she doesn't. Painters and paintings aren't on your mind; it is her you think of. And so you follow her as she leads you through the crowd.

Passing between starched and bedazzled bodies, you hear the shift in conversation: this to that, and then a bit mentioning Marie Antoinette, of which you know something about (you don't know how). You stop, but Rinette urges you on. You say, no. And, please. Wait for me, and you turn. Though blinded by what dangles from wrists, necks, and earlobes, you push your way through the crowd and say, "Lost her head—lopped clean off." You're proud of the step you make, truly, so smile. The men and women only stare. They say nothing. They look to one another then back to you, and laughter comes next. Had you been funny?—You weren't meaning to be funny. How can you stop this?—You don't know, so blush; you hate how you blush. You try and hide it. You rub one cheek then the other then your chin. You wipe the end of your nose then trace the rim of the glass you hold. You look over your shoulder; where's Rinette? She pushes past a couple engaged in heavy petting, and she steps between you and the laughing bunch. And you realize then the topic had changed—to what—your two cents did not afford:—something about something and some Wolf woman.

Rinette has positioned herself center, and all the painted faces laugh still, smoke spilling out their mouths and noses. Your throat tickles then catches; and you cough. You cough while the group holds their sides and slap each other's backs. Rinette's hands are at her hips, and one foot sticks far out from the planted other. "As if she didn't lose her head," Rinette says. (You don't know what this means.) You stuff your hands deep into your pockets. Did what Rinette say mean anything at all?—No matter, for you wife has the group's attention all the same.

"You all can choke on a silver spoon—hell, the whole damn dining set: forks, knives—all of it," Rinette says, then takes your hand out from you pocket and leads you from the silent bunch, whose cigarettes hang limp from their mouths.

"You did not have to do that," you say, though thankful she had. You keep the thought to yourself.

"Come on," she says, "I have something to show you."

* * *

A thick haze of smoke settles all around, masking all the pretty, pretty faces of the men and women who dance in place, swaying back and forth, moving to the sound of voices coming up and over the piano playing on. Bright, shiny grins show through, in concert with the doll-like eyes that are the holes of the lazy gray fog, which carries on—staining coats and fur trims.

"This is what I wanted to show you," Rinette says.

"Really, you didn't have to do what you did."

"Forget it, Garland. To lose sleep over those who've lost their sense of civility is to beat yourself up for having sneezed."

"Thank you," you say.

Rinette kisses your cheek, your forehead, and the tip of your nose.

"Here," she says. "This. This is it. An American painted it. Have a look."

You do.

"He was ahead of the Pop curve." He was very Bohemian, she says. His hair was as white as any snowflake she ever saw. Andy Warhol is the name, but it doesn't stick. You're stuck still on Bohemian. He was quite the socialite, she tells you, and the names that follow are: Liza Minnelli, Elizabeth Taylor, and Judy Garland. You know nothing about any of that, so mention you've seen The Wizard of Oz. Rinette thinks you are being funny. You blush as you had before, and you tell her you are joking and she should go on because she is on a roll. She does, and you drink from your drink. You drink and listen to your wife's cadence. It reminds you of the wind chimes you had as a child. In storms they would sing. Rinette sings. In a room so full you are calm.

The painting Rinette shows you has the title: Marilyn. It is very yellow, very pink, and very much something you have no idea how to describe.

"I like it," you say. You do, too, but you don't know why. You just do. Rinette says something you don't understand:—"Aesthetically pleasing." And you tell her sure, and yes; that's what you mean. You think it has something to do with the smile, but it is sad and empty, so you hope to hell it is not it at all.

"Listen to this," she says, and Rinette's tongue flicks when she says the word this. You are not as interested in the painting as you are in the way her tongue flicks. She tells you the painter was thought to have been quite sexual, though—most likely—a virgin up to the day he died. " . . . Blam-O. Shot in the guts."

"How exciting," you say.

"Very," she says then continues. "It was a loony who did it." The loony was a woman. She came in out from the dumpsters of New York. She thought she knew something about something and all the soup cans the very sexual painter painted, and so shot him—through and through. Blood and guts everywhere, Rinette says. You know something about that; the military has made sure of it. So you nod and smile and drink from the glass you have.

"Sounds very sticky," you say. "Tough clean up."

Rinette slaps you. Some of the time she is very playful, and you like this. She makes a gun then; she makes it out of her hand and fingers. And she pulls the trigger that is her thumb. Bang-bang, she says. You clutch your heart and go to your knees. You tell her she has got you. And she blows on the business end of her finger then holsters it. "Cleanup on aisle five," she says. The two of you are very dramatic. This excites you, and you tell her to go on, to describe all the gore she can.

"The story does not end there," she says.

Go on, you say.

"He would have turned in his chips, right then and there—that is if the loony had had any real idea as to what she was doing."

"Did she not aim?" You have to, you say, because you know something about that, about guns and aiming, about having a steady hand.

"No. No. No. It's not that. It's just, well, the loony had no clue as to why she was pulling the trigger. She did it because of something her mind made up. It was all very superficial. There was no truth to it, and so the painter went on kicking for a few years after—on and on—before meeting his maker. Natural causes or something like it—nothing too exciting." Rinette shakes her head then combs her hair, she pushes it behind her ears, and it falls onto her shoulders and on down her back.

"It must be sad to die a shell. I might just cry a whole damn river for the poor bastard that can no longer excite any great madness."

You see Rinette hears the music playing. Her toe taps, and she breaks into a song and dance; she circles around you and sings:

"There once was a white haired man/ who painted Campbell's soup cans/ he dabbled in smut/ and was shot in the guts/ sadly, his name's a forgotten brand."

You take her hand in yours and spin her; she spins, and her dress flairs, as blossoming orchids do. But she is looking back; her attention is taken. She stares at the smiling painting. "Really," she says, "now that I think about it, it might have actually been the starvation that snuffed out the painter."

You let her up; her dress flattens. You ask what she means.

She fingers the picture frame. "He had it in his head, to validate what he had done, he had to do away with food altogether." He could no longer look himself in the mirror and recognize the man staring back, she says. It is a matter of being able to look yourself in the mirror. He had it in his head he was not worth a damn, and having your guts shot meant you were. Bullets had not whizzed by his head in some time so he starved himself to make sense of his life . . . And though he most truly believed he would outlast us all, even he gave in to the pain of being forgotten by those who once stood by his side, who clapped his back, who said, Brilliant. Not even Basquiat could paint him out of the situation. "Kaput," Rinette says, "and like that, his heart stopped—gave up."

You want to cry right then and there.

A glass falls.

Your attention is taken.

The glass has shattered in the middle of all the men and women doing the Charleston. The glass pieces are kicked and stepped on, and the pretty, painted faces laugh and clap and cheer. The pianist's head and shoulders drop, and he sighs. His chin rests on his chest, and he breathes deep, settles, and returns to the piano keys once more, filling the room with song.

You recall then an author you had read some time ago, and how he, too, had wrapped his mouth around the business end of a double-barreled gun. You don't know why you recall this; you just do. And you wonder then if it is anything like the starvation the Bohemian did. You drink your drink.

Hemingway stared down the barrel once, you say. It was the only time he would. His first and last, you say. He blew his brains clear out of his skull.

"How exciting," Rinette says.

"I figure," you say, "he must have met the day he could no longer cut the mustard." He could not get in the ring—not any more—and if he did, he would be out the first round. "I figure it was the day he hung his gloves for good, and after, he turned out the lights."

Rinette catches a passing server and asks whether he has a napkin. He does. He hands it to her, and she hands it to you. The server asks if she would care for a cigarette: filtered, non-filtered, menthol—whatever. No. No. No, Rinette says. "Too much time's wasted smoking," she says. The server bows and says very well. "It is a shield," Rinette says, which she aims more your way than the server's. "It's not healthy to hide behind clouds." The server has gone, and you are left holding the napkin your wife has given you. "This is your chance," she says. And she produces a pen and tells you to take it and to write her six little words, to write her a story. Go ahead, Hemingway.

You have never written any story, though knowing a correspondent once. He had been in the same platoon as you. His name you forget. He wrote of war, of women losing men. You never could stomach a word he wrote. Each was death. So you write the first thing that comes to mind. You write: Love. Loss. And so it goes. It is the first story you have ever written; and you realize you have become the man whose name you forget. And it kills you.

"Well, Ernest, blow me away."

"It's nothing, really."

Rinette takes the napkin from you and reads what you have written. She turns it over and kisses the back. "If we want," she says, "we can dance around in our underpants." Rinette then glues the napkin to the painting, which carries still the empty, wretched smile.

It is something sad, but Rinette tells you differently. It is not sad, she says, not at all. Life has its pattern; it's repeating. You have summed it up, she says, with your six little words. "Life on repeat, because that's all it takes."

"Now don't go and make any ant into an elephant."

Rinette extends an arm and waves it about as if she had a trunk of her own.

"Call me Dumbo and I will never forget it." Rinette hugs you from behind. She stands on her toes and rests her chin on your shoulder, her trunk-arm, too. Together, you face the napkin and stare.

"Feed me a peanut and I will follow you forever."

You tickle her hanging fingertips; and Rinette coos. "There are some," she says, "those that forget. They forget life's repeating. They lose sight of the fact: It is made up of a pattern, and it goes on and on." Those who lose sight turn out all the lights.

"Ants forget," she says, "and everyday they're stepped all over—crushed beneath passing feet."

"Am I an ant?"

"No one has to be. Look. See. We have ourselves a reminder." Rinette points.

You take her earlobe between your thumb and forefinger and rub it.

"Tell me something nice," you say. "Say something pretty."

Okay. "Slamming into a tree was Pollock's most personal work. His mess spoke to the human condition."

"Are we morbid?" Your voice has softened.

"Not at all," she says then blows on the back of your neck; you like this.

"Then what?"

"The way I see it: Pollock, Hemingway, and Warhol, too—they all threw in the towel too soon. Their stories ended on notes of loss. They had forgotten the pattern." Rinette points once more to the napkin. "For any story to be successful there must be gain."

"Then why do we dig up the dead? I don't want to think we are only spreading ash."

No. No. No. Their loss is our gain. "Ours," she says. They painted such pretty examples.

"And what do those examples say?"

"To love and do diddlysquat about it is to go on tying shoes and reading the Sunday funnies, thinking all the while what a terrific feeling you had once. It is to go on and plow yourself into some tree, as Pollock had, making a great mess of yourself."

* * *

Rinette pulls you onto the dance floor, and though you had done a little jig, and you had dipped and spun her before, you resist now. "I was fine right where I was," you say. "I have two left feet. Wait. No. I have the strange feeling any minute my appendix might burst."

Rinette smiles.

"Nonsense," she says, and "Your feet are just fine," and "In case you haven't noticed, your appendix has been AWOL for some time now."

"But—"

"But nothing. We are dancing."

Rinette circles and twirls and spins and sings:

"There once was a Dutch Impressionist/ whose sadness was his antagonist/ his head had not cleared/ so lopped off an ear/ and after, with a gun, spelled: Masochist."

Her voice carries. She moves right, and you, too. Her feet step left, and yours follow. Again and again, and you are dancing. You are Fox Trotting. Rinette quickens, and you chase after. She lets you take the lead, which you like very much. You take her into a Cha-Cha number you picked up some time ago, and Rinette's head goes back; her hair has fallen past her shoulders and behind, swinging free like a sheet in the wind. She smiles, as she does, and she leans into your hands that hold her hips. Her arms are around what she says is not such a roughneck, and again she breaks into song. You listen. Her melody rises as all else does: the piano, the clinking of glasses, the clapping of backs, and what you imagine to be a group of slick adjuncts who carry on—throwing about stats, names, and titles—which they immediately retract after a passing man stops. And Rinette sings on, but the stopped man's barking draws your attention. You hear: "Erroneous," which comes between your wife's interlude and humming. And the young, fine-combed men are broken; you don't have to see to know.

Rinette trails. And you hear what is said next, what comes from the mouth of the barking man, who's sipping a highball and smoking a cigar. "Gibberish," he says. "All which you call research has become the bubbling pustule that festers on the backside of even the most mediocre of accredited institutes. You are all fools for buying stock in such poppycock. Flimflam. The man was and is a phony."

You prefer Rinette's singing to all of it:—to those who insist on making a dance floor a battleground. It is a sad thing to see and hear a gang go to pieces, to imagine their boots being blown off. There is nothing comical about it. There is nothing funny in seeing a bunch of sad-faced men picking up what is left of their bootstraps. You know this so step around the broken glass. You turn Rinette under the light that shines down. And her face glows, brighter than anything you know; you like it very much. And you think: She is all you need, will ever need to brighten a room.

Please. Please. Please. Sing another, you say.

She does, too:

"A day flower, a mayflower—nothing will grow. Not a gillyflower, or a Lilly flower—if ignoring Van Gogh. P.S. Sorry. Sorry."

* * *

Rinette presses her cheek to yours. Her body pushes into you, and you hear her breathe. You hear your name called. And you turn. You spin on your toes. Rinette follows as if thinking you are taking her for another Cha-Cha number, or—maybe—for a little Waltz bit because she likes it so much.

"Was that you? I heard my name being called."

"Oh Garland. Garland. Garland."

"No. Really—"

Again the voice comes. And you recognize it. It barks.

The man passes through the cloud that swallows the party whole— all that glitters. Through his mouth and nose he breathes a cloud of his own. The end of his cigar glows red-orange-yellow. Out of his mouth, it hangs. It bounces with every pull he takes, up and down; one and two. His face flickers. His eyes flash. They are blue and cold looking. And they peer through the rising plume of grey-white, which spills out from his grinning face. He extends his hand. It breaks the fog, and he is clear: clean-shaven, his suit well pressed, and his shoes shine. His glass is empty. "Without a doubt," he says. "Unmistakable. The Great Garland Starkweather . . . To what do I owe the pleasure?"

You ask whether Rinette knows the man.

"Oh—"

"How absolutely rude of me. Allow me to introduce myself. William Burgess, PhD. Hasn't Nettie told you? Our offices share a common wall."

You exchange a nervous glance with your wife. And she is biting her nails, and you know this is a man she does not like, who she is not comfortable around; you don't need for her to explain this for you to know it to be true. Her eyes say enough;—so much so—you know (by her waning verve) William has become something of a throbbing pain, something sharp in her side; and his presence only furthers the feeling of continual thorn pricks.

"Come now. I won't bite. Take my hand. Don't make me out to be the fool."

You have positioned yourself between William and Rinette. You take his hand and shake it; his grip is strong. You let it be.

The man looks past you, stilling holding your hand in his. "Nettie, and why is it you haven't mentioned it's to the Garland Starkweather you're married." Still the two of you shake. And he pulls you close. Your chests touch. William wears the smell of Scotch whisky, as a woman would perfume. You swallow the urge to cough.

"I see you have found yourself quite the prize. Cheers to you, Mr. Starkweather. To you and your sparkling reward."

Your noses touch.

"Be very careful with what you say next."

"How ever did you two meet?"

* * *

You are young again—twenty or so; and neon lights flicker ahead. You have had a day in the field, so you think to take to the local bar. Its sign glows against the flat, night sky. Inside is dark and smoky. You dig at your ear; a ringing has settled there. Mortars had gone off earlier, and guns were all about—firing and spitting flames, lighting the heavens above, red-yellow. The explosions are with you still, beating about and drumming. Pounding. Will it last?—Is war all the time?—No matter where, when? You pull up to the bar and order a drink. The bartender says it is on the house and he thanks you. You nod and thank him. A girl sits nearby. It is Rinette, (a student still) but you do not know this yet. She is delicate, fair, and soft looking. She is not alone; a man in tweed stands over, looking down on her. Words come from his mouth, but you cannot make them out, for bells are ringing. You do see how they affect her, though. He grabs her by the arm. And what comes over you, you don't know. It comes all the same, and that's all. "You have dunged-up the place," you say then box the man's nose. And you wind up for another round; you want another round. But the man has fallen. So you turn to where you realize Rinette has lost her balance. She is falling, too. You go to your knees and catch her before she hits the ground. And your noses touch.

"I can never trust a man who is in camp with Gauguin or Rivera," she says, and her arms hang about your neck. You like this very much. Her breath breaks across you. And you are warm.

"What?" you say then dig at your ear. "Oh, well, I know nothing about that, but I do know something about treating a woman fine."

"You have ruined me, solider. And I might just love you forever."

* * *

Rinette calls your name. It's all that keeps you from figuring whether William is willing to lose and arm, hand, or nose—if he would care to wear his testicles for a hat, because you know something about breaking a man; you do not want to, but will.

"I do hope Nettie has found better use of her time. Those finger paintings are such a waste, such a childish pastime."

"I think it's time for you to go," you say.

"And why should I, Mr. Starkweather?"

"Garland," Rinette says, "Please. We should go. Leave him be." Rinette pulls at your coat. And she pulls at your arm. She shakes your shoulder. "It's not worth it," she says.

"Mr. Starkweather is going nowhere," William says, and he whispers into your ear: "I know who you really are."

"Hold your tongue," you say.

"Does your wife know? Does she know how you choked? You are a coward," he says then stands back, straightens, sucks down a lungful of cigar smoke and blows a ringed cloud your way, which rises then splits in two.

You hold your breath, keep your mouth tight, and chew the fat of your cheek. You know what he's referring to—what he means, and like many others, he has it all wrong.

War had broken (years ago, when you were young—college age—before meeting Rinette) and the draft had come. It was in full affect. You were given a deferment then, like some others, those that had one thing or another going for them, which kept them from picking up any gun, from being shipped off across the Atlantic, from being forced to fight. For you (specifically) it was said you had on you a "golden arm," to which you had no reply; you never really understood it. It was all very Hollywood sounding, as you saw it at least, so took to it not so well. Slick magazines, sports journals, newspapers, and so on all reported your football exploits, you "heroics": Starkweather Throws, Yet Another, Million Mile Touchdown Pass, etc., etc. Starkweather Believed To Take The Big Game—All Rides On Him. Bets were made, sure, but it was no care of yours, really. You thought little of it, for your thoughts were on the war.

You had come across an article, hours before the game you were slated to appear as starting quarterback, titled: Our Fathers and Brothers—The Real Heroes. You read it, and after, looked to the uniform you were told to wear. It was then you realized the uniform was no uniform at all—nothing but a jersey you would end up passing off once too old to carry. You realized also, the field a soldier fought on was nothing like yours—not at all. No stadium. No crowds cheering and clapping—none of that. The whole world had a ticket to your show then, watching either in person or on the television, and all the while the real fighting—the real heroics took place off cameras, off the side-lines where there was no cheering, no half-times. You made up your mind then, after having read the article: Real heroics are the things you do, the fighting—whatever, when no one is looking.

You had heard your name called and all the cheering that echoed throughout the stadium, but that was no matter. You did not answer. You left the stadium without ever taking to the field. To hell with deferments, you said, and after, enlisted.

"You choked," William says again.

"I will sleep better knowing I was never your hero."

"Hero?" William laughs then pushes his finger into you. "What's with the uniform, anyway? You're no fighter." William looks over your shoulder once more. "Who's he fighting for, Nettie? You? He couldn't cut the mustard then and he can't—"

You take William's finger and bend it back; he buckles. His glass falls. It shatters. Yours you still have. William cries out. His cigar falls. And he whimpers. Smoke rises from the bruised hardwood floor.

"You are done here," you say.

"I—"

"I'm only going to say this once. I'm going to let you go and you are going to walk away. You will not speak to my wife or me ever again, unless—that is—it's to tip your hat, or to say 'what nice weather we're having.' Anything more and I will make damn sure you never wag this finger again. You'll have a hell of a time wiping your backside. Get me? Do you understand?"

You let William go.

William nurses his arm, his hand, his finger; he cradles them.

"You have gone dry," you say. "Go and have yourself another drink because I know you need it. But be on your way."

The man stares at the glittering floor, at his flattened cigar, at his shinning shoes—decorated on all sides by broken glass.

"Yes. It seems I have spilled my drink. How clumsy of me. What a fool I am."

"And now, say 'goodnight.'"

"Yes. Yes. Goodnight, Mr. and Mrs. Starkweather."

William shambles off and fades into the crowd of pretty, pretty faces, and the piano plays on.

"You did not have to do that," Rinette says.

"I did."

"I know." Rinette pauses. "Garland, really, I don't know what I would ever do if something were to happen to you. I might go to pieces . . . right here, in this very spot—I'm sure of it."

"It's nothing to lose sleep over."

"Garland?"

"Yes."

"Promise me one thing."

"Anything."

"Promise me you'll stick around."

"Always." And you pull Rinette close. You pull her into you. You kiss her hard. Her lips are soft, and they are wet. You do not think about screwing. No. "Listen," you say. "I have an early march tomorrow so have to turn in. Are you staying?—Will you be fine, here?"

"Yes. Yes, of course. Big, big parties are nice like that: They are one thing one minute and another the next; what a lovely atmosphere."

"Wake me when you get in?"

"Of course . . . Oh, as if I miss you already."

"Trust me. I'll stick around."

"Go then, because I know you'll be there when I come calling."

"And when you come calling, sing won't you."

"I will, Garland. I will."

"That's good, for when all's gone to hell, your voice makes sense of it all."

And Rinette grins—the way she does. It tells you everything is fine and good. And you believe it because nothing says otherwise.

* * *

Paralyzed, you cannot escape the smoke that's all around, filling the kitchen from floor to ceiling, and all its corners. You cough, and the gun shifts beneath you.

"Garland, please say something. Anything. Speak, please."

You pull your hand from Rinette's and cover your mouth and nose, and cough again and again; you are choking. How can you make it stop?

"Forget about the toaster," Rinette says, and she waves her hand in its direction.

"Please, just throw it out," you say between hacking. "Do away with it. It's broken. It has gone to pieces."

"Nonsense," Rinette says, and "All it needs is a little work and a close eye," and "It's perfectly fine the way it is."

"But I don't want the toast to burn. Not yours, anyway."

Rinette reaches again across the table that separates you two; she pulls your hand from your mouth and nose and takes it in hers, brings it close and cups it. And you are touching, really.

"It won't happen," she says. "I won't let it. We won't let it."

Between the microwave oven and the refrigerator the toaster goes up in flames: red-orange-yellow, all spitting from its insides. And Hopper's painting glows; it's on fire.

"Fire," you say.

"Let it alone."

And in Rinette's eyes you see more fire. It reflects. But it's not fire at all. It's something else—something different. And you realize, all the painters, all the canvases hanging about—everything—you have painted them out to be something more. But not really, some kind of fancy clothes you hide behind. For beneath them—under it all is the heart of the matter; you had not seen it before. You couldn't; you wouldn't allow yourself. You were afraid. And because of it you adopted some queer world in which you isolated yourself. So it is your head, not your wheelchair that has become your prison—where you feel most alone, so small. And it is that loneliness you created that got you in the worst of ways. You now realize you have painted a world for yourself, in which you have become lost—apart from your wife, Rinette. It is a world of fancy disguises, consisting of painters, paintings, and authors—whatever. And in Rinette's eyes you see that; you see that beneath it all it's just you and her—nothing more. For all that matters is sitting here, at the kitchen table, burning before you. And you are warm. Not because of the fire, and not like the barrel of the gun that sits beneath you. For it is not warm at all. The gun is not warm because you couldn't fire it, but because you didn't fire it—

"Let's do away with all the paintings," you say. "The big ones, the small ones, and the medium-sized ones, too. We don't need them. They don't matter."

"But I like them."

"I know you do, too. And there's a part of me that wants you to have more, as many as your heart desires, but we don't need them."

"I know, but they do brighten the room."

"And it's good that they do, but we can find something new—something fresh—something that doesn't bring just the room together."

"I think we can find something like that."

"I am positive we can," you say, knowing you have already seen how Rinette's face flickers.

Rinette then stands. She passes through the kitchen's fog. She does not stop at the burning toaster. She continues on but slips. She loses her footing on the spilt butter. You turn in your wheelchair and catch her before she falls and hits the ground. And your noses touch.

"I do believe you have ruined me, soldier. And I think I might love you forever."

"I'm no hero. And I'm no soldier."

"No. No heroics—just you. All that I need."

And the fire alarm beeps and sounds wildly; and the sprinkler kicks then spurts. Water falls from above, as if it were raining. It's the coolness of the rain that convinces you that you are being cleansed—washed of sadness, pain, and concern—of everything too big for words, too much to say aloud. And that's fine. All's gone and passed now. You know this because Rinette has put her arms around you. She holds you close. And her head rests on your chest. You feel her heart beating and her breathing slow, and she lets out a soft sigh, as if to say, she too knows everything is fine and good—everything will be okay. She rises, though, but not to leave.

Rinette crosses the kitchen as she had before; this time stepping around the spilt butter, to take the two slices of bread from the blackened toaster. She plates the two pieces and returns; she pulls up beside you. "I like it when there's a bit of a crunch," she says. "It's a texture thing." The toast is black all over, and steam comes up off the plates as more rain falls, pitter-pattering on the tabletop, the floor tiling—all around. "You're a lovely cook," you say. "I couldn't ask for anyone better."

"Oh, stop it," Rinette says. "You're being fresh."

"I'll never stop, ever—I can't." And you don't want to either. "Rinette?" you say.

"Yes."

"Crack the window, won't you. Open it all the way. It's not well of us to take in so much smoke."

"Not at all," she says. "We might just croak, right here and now, that is before we're ever given the chance to cough up a lung."

Rinette opens the window nearest the refrigerator, and all the smoke that had gathered escapes in a rush; all the while a damp cool, morning breeze fills the kitchen, which leaves you with goose pimples racing up your hands and arms. But you do not shiver; you're not cold. All is steady and right. You look to Rinette, who is at the windowsill, looking out onto the street below, and the sun hits her face. She glows. And her hair lifts, taken by the calm wind coming from the outside, and it is a stream of yellow, which trails gently behind her.

"Come," you say. "Have a seat with me. Here in my lap."

Rinette does.

"Would you look at that," she says, combing the flattened whiskers that grow out your chin. "Your beard is coming in."

"I hate it," you say.

"Oh, Garland. Please, please keep it. It's very rugged, you know—very manly." And Rinette lifts her arms and flexes them. She sucks in her cheeks then puckers her lips. She growls and shows her teeth, and she laughs. "Very manly," she says. "I like it. Keep it, please."

"Okay. I'll keep it, because you like it. But you'll have to do something for me."

"Anything. Anything."

"Won't you sing for me? There never was a sweeter voice."

"Wait," she says. "I have an idea." And Rinette kicks her legs around and stands. "Write me a story. No—tell me a story. Please. Your mind works so wonderfully, so beautifully . . . Cook something up real nice, something that'll make my head throb like a heart. No one tells a story like you. No one . . . Most only muscle through it, but not you; your stories are plain and true. No nonsense."

"Okay. Okay. But don't go mad, for all I have is about six words in me."

"You'd be crazy to have any more."

Rinette then pushes you from the kitchen to the bedroom, which you allow. And you don't think about screwing, or the gun. You simply say, "Would you like me to say it straight, or sing it?"

"Oh, please, please, please won't you sing it."

"Okay—"

"Wait. Let me get comfortable."

Rinette settles down in your lap and pulls her legs tight to her chest, and she curls into a ball where she closes her eyes and rests her head on your shoulder, as if to fall asleep right there. "It's just you and me," she says. "Us against a world well lost."

And you sing:

Love. Loss. And so it goes.

About Benjamin R. Hostetter

"I am a recent VCU graduate, with a degree in English. I live in Richmond, Va, where I write everyday, and where I live also with my dog, F. Scott Fitzgerald, Scotty for short."

The Inhuman Fashion

by Mark Wagstaff

Some men aren't really at ease in jeweler shops. Middle-age, mid-range men who call necklaces 'nice' and rings 'kinda shiny'; who couldn't name more than five gemstones, and have never heard of carnelian nor what makes it semi-precious. Real wiseguys working the line maybe, they just know in jeweler shops they'll get scalped.

Mr. Rawsthorn was very much in that quarter. A semi-paid-for fixer-upper he had views on jewelry not shared by Mrs. Rawsthorn whose unnumbered Special Birthday cajoled his trip to the store. He stood looking in the window, a kid forbidden candy, tossing around in his mind if jeweler displays were still paste fakes and what chance he'd be sold a paste fake and never know but his wife would. He didn't want to get her birthday wrong again.

He was not reassured by the sales assistant: a polished young miss who looked born for discreetly heartstopping rocks at ears and throat. She knew a lot about jewels, and the office guys in effortless suits knew the book on creaming commission.

Aiming on minimal humiliation Mr. Rawsthorn pitched for earrings. Small, not too flashy, thoughtfully unostentatious; wouldn't prompt a change of wardrobe. In trays beneath display cases lit like showgirls' bathrooms lay row on row of diamond tears, pearl raindrops, ruby pools of frozen forensic. The assistant asked what Mrs. Rawsthorn was like, what did she like, what hues and looks did she favor. A lot of men wouldn't know but Mr. Rawsthorn, as the man getting asked, felt aggrieved, tricked; his lunch hour wasted, he ponied for diamonds, guessing no woman could argue with that. Took the girl twenty minutes to tissue wrap and box 'em.

Mrs. R was charmed at the box, adored the tissue wrap, thought the gems on their doll house cushion looked a dream. A damn-on perfect marital moment, spoiled only when her middle-age but still smooth fingers fumbled round under the padding and the unsheathed butterfly stabbed her thumb. As blood devastated caramel linen she glossed it as accidental. But Mr. Rawsthorn felt numbly to blame for another birthday wrecked.

Septicemia is no respecter of class nor personal grooming. It carries off people from all zones of the scale and often improbably. My ex-wife's kid sister caught eternity rubbing her elbow raw on nylon matting. I thought about that when Mr. Rawsthorn came to see me, right after the police told him if he called again he was theirs for the night. That something - when a mild guy gets a bite of extreme anger -

is more absorbing and almost clownishly harsh than a tough head breaking to tears. Restless in my dirty office air he got more anger than his body could contain. Not because his wife was dead. Because she was gone.

That was the part that struck him off the police goodwill list. He wanted his wife interred and not unreasonably felt short-changed to get handed a cookie jar filled with dust and a line about misfiling at the morgue. He didn't think loved ones should vanish so simply. We traded paranoia and I made fun of him when he left purely because my secretary got a hot laugh.

Coupla weeks later, painting doughnut grease on the news pages, I fell in on a sad little story. A girl - just a kid - killed at the rink and when her folks went to the funeral home to finalize arrangements they were told her body got mashed by foxes that somehow dug in the chiller. None too pretty after, the guys voted to screw the lid down. But what really put my pants on was a gag my secretary found. This stiff on his way to make compost when a family rift caused dispute round ownership of the plot. Long-to-short the guy got exhumed except - my girl cackled - when they cracked the box they eyeballed a heap of old Henry James, who it seemed was now no longer required reading. A dead guy somehow changed to rotting books.

First brush of the fashion I didn't even feel it. Lars Marling, the only guy I knew who got his picture in ink without the words 'Police net tightens...' for a strapline, ran those arty start-ups where drunching and cocktail maneuvers laid the turf. Marling's crowd got fashionably drunk the way regular guys get stinking. I knew him respectably from my whitewashing certain transactions the Constitution gives me freedom not to detail. In return I caught RSVPs on parties where business got dealt. Chance to practice my social skills, like the blonde who claimed she was a definite pencil for some airhead movie. I don't recall her face but remember her pitch how she was so hot for the part where she was ahead on the fashion. Said it real pushy: the fashion, like maxing some new party drug.

My ex-wife's kid sister watched TV, chilling on this matting floor. Without thinking I guess she propped on her elbows maybe five, six hours a day. Just mild, constant abrasion. Septicemia. She sure liked TV. Mr. Rawsthorn seemed surprised I hadn't kept his business card and it would have felt low to give him false hope if that wasn't key to my job spec. The office guys in the jeweler shop really didn't like me, seeing cheap in a man who throws a look on random rocks and claims they're perfect. I never seen a chick so surly with tissue wrap.

Right before my tired plastic got bilked I made a big hoo-ee on checking the goods; a nimble finger ahead of hers leveraged the cushion. The clip shone needle sharp. I asked - I thought pleasantly -

ought there to be stoppers on that. One of the guys beetled out the glass booth: I got a swift change of heart and left him chewing his gums at the window.

My secretary was crap words a minute typing, her shorthand so crap she made up signs she couldn't remember what for. She preferred strong liquor, jokes about death and infertility, loaned me money; sometimes let me maul her round, so I wouldn't feel wretched. She was thirty-two, divorced, called herself Lucinda Brannan. She got inducted into flashback by a high velocity hunting rifle off the roof cross the street. A clean, efficient act.

I didn't need that to know the police are wiseguys and mortician ain't a job you kinda drift into. The first I already discovered; the second don't need working out. I made arrangements quickly - thanks to her savings account - fretful some family might show and take her from me. She got shot so well when they cleaned her up and dressed her and flossied her with some paste jewelry the hole in her head looked no more than a mild inconvenience. The prissy young man who prepped her out gave me no cause to misunderstand how his stiffs were in fashion.

Mr. Rawsthorn pained me, called me up though we weren't contractually related. He got the notion that blood poisoning and morgue employment of illiterate monkeys were fields I could swing some dick in, happy not to get paid. It was respite from his civilian self-regard persuaded me on Marling's invitation to some hippy place down a dirt road mostly travelled by horny toads. Country air, the shock of silence made me pull over, look out on a few hundred miles of nothing and doubt I could break my recent habit of sleeping with the lights on.

The spread was owned by a jaw named Glock Hinterstroder who maybe with reason went by Johnny. Kinda guy who wears his dressing gown over a dinner shirt. His guests were moneyed trash, porn stars and interns; guys I recognized from technicality acquittals. There wasn't much to do but it was done classy. I don't play tennis; I'm self-conscious when I swim, and there's only so much juve ass a bereaved man can handle. So mostly I mooched, like always. From unpromising terrain Johnny fashioned his place to country club values: smart and knowing, firmly grounded in rights of self-defense. The plugs in boiled collars on the gate weren't serving drinks.

He got a lake of Chinese ducks, a yard of Arab racers, a few little hobbyist sheds dotted round where houseguests could play Versailles while waiting for their hangover cure. That one shed got its door locked was bound to tweak my tail. Window mesh stopped the glass from getting cleaned; dark inside, my eyes not what they were, it could easy have been a store house. But I got a jumpy nature: nagging shapes in the dusty murk kept me looking back and back, shielding my eyes, pressed on the mesh, breaking all pretence at sleuthing to try figure inside the gloom. The familiarity of what I was looking at hit me with surprised embarrassment, a shock doubled by the hand on my shoulder that had me halfway to Mars.

Even if I thought Johnny a pleasant fellow before, the warmth of his smile and hand on my back got me checking my wallet and kidneys. I asked kinda hearty if guests could try tailoring along with other old-school pastimes. He murmured - the guy only murmured - that he could get it arranged. Trapped in a hole of my own digging I said that's what I thought the shed of showroom dummies was for. He murmured could be: if his friends yearned to play needle'n'chalk they might get to use his collection.

As a kid, sure I hung out as much as anyone outside big store windows speculating on the physical form of plastic mannequins. But for a guy who could buy a ride wholesale, it seemed kinda retro to hoard the things in a locked shed. He laid a big finger against my lips - tasted cold, kinda waxy - said not to spoil the fun.

After dinner we got corralled in one of Johnny's gazillion sitting rooms, gathered relaxed and easy, his goons on point by the doors. Mr. Hinterstroder told us this was some momentous day, truly revelatory when we would be first to see what was new for the city.

Behind a flush-fit door Johnny led us into a gallery: no windows, candles throwing Halloween shapes on linenned walls. There was a party going on. Jazz-lite slunk from speakers, glasses clinked in sound effect around tableau furniture draped and occasioned with figures. Seated and stood in attitudes of smalltalk and laughter, a frozen cocktail moment where the drink got poured, the line got pitched, the hit put on that would end someplace beyond midnight in silk sheets. Like any night at Marling's. But locked in stillness.

"These," Johnny murmured, "are inhumans."

Average height: around five-six to six-two; sized from slim to businesslike; mostly young but the waiters were old guys. Like storefront dolls with impressive bodywork: no seams, no moldings. Some cat asked if they got built 3D by lasers. Johnny liked that, said the technology was way more confrontational than a light show. Edgy, he said. Jagged edgy, feeling around some blonde statue that stared to the off-distance. Marling could barely contain his kid-at-the-air-crash glee, pestering our host for the good his toys could be put to.

In the present time - Johnny leaned relaxed on a stony waiter's shoulder - this exhibition was pretty much all they did. But he was thinking animatronics: from objets d'art to pliable associates, from static decoration to willingness. "Inhumans," he told us, "will soon be capable as you or me. But without issues of refusal."

Some wiseguy laughed why bother? Why not just drug real folks?

"That would be impolite."

I went to work Monday hungover, sour at wealthy screwballs; loathing each message Rawsthorn taped in his dark hours. Shocked how a desk slung with trash and hardened doughnut crumbs got left empty beside the door. Online, some guy was bitching his girl strayed on route to the graveyard, pissed on how he just paid for her engagement ring.

The inhuman fashion took quick hold any place a martini got shaken. Chinese styled inhumans appeared downstream of the food chain. Inhumans fronted blogs and Dear John pages. Though the animatronics were still kinda scratchy, inhuman porn was in its own style compelling.

Marling entrepreneured a good run of the fashion, though knowing the guy I guessed Hinterstroder's brain ticked behind Lars' shit-eating grin. Quicktime, inhumans traded up from the funny pages to must-haves on the red carpet. Some crackhead pop chick married one in Vegas. A lot of pious heat got talked about medical uses, inhumans giving comfort to the sick: steady, consistent, above all cheap patient care. Big hoo-ee. The market was decorative entertainment: no party was worth being late for that didn't have themed inhumans pouring drinks or turning tricks. Street-side, 'inhuman' was both cuss and high praise.

Lars Marling shot the best parties. Though slowing up a little I still showed, kidding myself there'd be tail or at least conversation to puncture a life that got as long as a hospital night. In borrowed clubs that took slack from his crowded apartment I spent more time with inhumans than most. Pretty meat dollies, all you could want made plasticized flesh and - the best part - so in fashion it didn't feel foul or lonesome spilling guts to their absent eyes. As zither music and shutout laughter filled the background, I stroked their construction, mussed their hair, held hands.

Lemme tell you about their hands. Some vintage models got lined and livered but mostly inhumans got mud-smooth hands, wintry and just a tad moist. Their production process discreet behind brick-faced lawyers it was technology so classy you liked an inhuman before you even met.

So at Lars' party, avoiding girls I'd never make, I took time for those strangely familiar flesh puppets. Getting juiced with a blonde too good for me, I stroked up her fingers the same how my ex said drove her crazy. I stopped, puzzled. I got a closer look. Her hands were smooth for sure but - some faint dissonance set nagging - I peered harder and finer at vinyl skin till I found a little pinprick hole on the ring finger.

I checked another: pierced ears; a male with a puncture positioned right for a collar stud; a female with residual redness where a bracelet might ride. All the inhumans in that room got some imperfection located for jewelry. Sure were a lot of jeweler shops opened up lately, and with prices so low we'd become a dazzling society. Clean living too: new hygiene laws got the dead tidied damn fast. We got used to goodbyes with the lid down.

Did I tell anyone? No. People get sick and sad, blame each other; the fashion for better than humans gave so much comfort. A steady supply, easily replaced when they got to look too familiar. One sour guy shouldn't tumble down that. It would be impolite.

About Mark Wagstaff

Mark Wagstaff is a British writer who since 1999 has had about 50 short stories published across a range of journals, anthologies and sites - details at www.markwagstaff.com . Mark's 2008 novel The Canal is available in ebook from Bristlecone Pine Press. His latest novel In Sparta, a story of radicalism, conformity and terror, is available in print or ebook from Troubador.

Los Malandros

by C. Osvaldo Gómez

Cesar's evening had gone well, really well. There was a wad of pesos in his pocket. Many new customers had come to his spot: the alley behind Lazaro's Cantina on Vicente Guerrero Boulevard. To celebrate, he pulled out a funnel tube and lighter from his pant pocket, and placed a small brown crystal on a piece of foil.

By the time Cesar entered the rehabilitation center, his temporary residence, he was floating on several hits of Mexican mud. The place was poorly lit. An old table lamp, its switch set on low, was meant to provide a safe welcome to the residents, regardless of how they returned; as extra precaution, each night, the attending counselor moved chairs and small furniture out of the hallway, in case residents came home intoxicated.

Cesar walked down the hallway feeling like he could walk through walls. As he neared the staff room, he felt the need to take deeper breaths. Not remembering who was on duty, Carmen or Felipe, he staggered toward his room. He'd felt great, but now a dull pain pulled on his chest from inside. Like the end of a movie scene, his eyes began fading to black, until there was total darkness.

Cesar opened his eyes the following day. Where am I? he asked himself, feeling nauseous. Throbbing pain was coming from his head. He touched where his head hurt; a piece of gauze was taped along the side of his forehead. He recognized the room, the faint-colored walls, painted with diluted yellow paint. He sat up on the bed, trying to figure out what happened. His pants were on the floor, by his tennis shoes and dirty socks. He stared at them, wondering. When he realized their importance, he jumped out of bed, and grabbed them, going for the pockets first, frantically pulling them inside out. Empty.

"Hey, hey, who's here right now?" he asked loudly. Pepe, a chubby kid of about ten years of age with skin the color of chocolate, ran in the room.

"You alright, Cesar?" he asked. "¿Que pasa?"

"They stole my money and my chiva, chingado."

"I don't know about any money, but your drug stuff is with Carmen. You know they're not allowed."

Cesar got out of bed slowly. His muscles ached as he slid his legs through the leg holes of his pants. He picked up his shirt from the ground, shook it for scorpions and dust, and put it on. His socks were dank. He smelled them; their foul odor caused him to quickly turn his face away. Dressed, he walked out of the bedroom, and down the hallway. Three young men sat in the living room, watching the soccer match between Pumas and America.

El títere (Puppet) munched on a straw, sitting with his chest to backrest on a chair. El búho (Owl) sat on a giant wooden spool, flicking the ear lobe of el Gringo, who wasn't a gringo, but looked so white he could pass for an American. One of these assholes must have taken my money, Cesar thought. As former El Paso gang-bangers and junkies, Puppet, Owl, and Gringo weren't afraid to search people. They would know where to look for cash, where to find hidden contraband. Out on the street the three would've taken everything from Cesar, his tennis shoes, pants, even his shirt. Since they couldn't easily hide clothing at the center, they'd cut Cesar a break and settled for the drugs and his money.

"You got my chiva?" Cesar said to Carmen, looking inside the room that had been converted to an office. Carmen, an obese, olive-tanned twenty-year-old, looked up from behind the monitor of a ten-year-old Gateway desktop. She stared at him incredulously.

"How about a 'thank-you' to go with that attitude?"

"What?" he asked, irritably.

"You almost died last night, Cesar. You overdosed on street heroin."

"What about the money? It was taken out of my pockets, damn it. I had four thousand pesos when I got here."

"Aren't you listening? The doctor had to administer two doses of naloxone to keep you breathing through the night...said you would have died for sure if you had injected the crap."

Cesar was unmoved.

"When the doctor and I went through your pockets, all we found was your pipe."

"It's not a pipe. It's a funnel tube."

"Whatever...here," she said, pulling the tube out of the top desk drawer, disappointed he'd used again after a month sober. "Get rid of it."

"Pinchi bola de rateros," (fucking bunch of thieves) he said, snatching the pipe from her corpulent hand.

"Pepe stayed by you the whole night. You're his favorite you know!"

I don't care, he thought. I didn't ask him to. He hadn't asked to be saved from death either. At twenty, Cesar figured he'd lived long enough, longer than he had expected to, so every day was like finding money in the pocket of an old coat, a surprise. He enjoyed living on the edge, recklessly. High on drugs, he felt alive, powerful, and unaffected by pain or struggle.

Cesar was slim, and his skin complexion was the color of vanilla. Hyper wasn't a temporary condition; it was who he was, always on the move. He had a one-inch scar below his right ear, an injury he sustained from a knife fight at sixteen. After the fight, everyone Cesar knew began calling him, "Scarface."

Cesar was smart. "There's no limit to what you can accomplish, mijo," his mother said to him on his thirteenth birthday. She died from a crack overdose the following day. All that mattered to Cesar, after his mother's passing, was surviving alone in the world. The streets of Juarez were tough. For protection, and the brotherly love he desired, Cesar joined a gang of other street thugs, other malandros like him. Glue, mescaline, alcohol, marijuana, heroin, tobacco, he did it all, accompanied by his homies, in the bitter winter cold as flakes of snow fell from the sky, white as cocaine, in the dry summer heat, with chapped lips, broken skin, and little volcanoes on his forearms.

"Where's my money, putos?" Cesar asked Puppet, Owl, and Gringo.

They looked at Cesar with indifference.

"What money?" Puppet asked. Owl and Gringo stayed quiet, allowing Puppet to speak for them.

"La feria you stole from me, cabrón."

"We ain't got your feria," Puppet said, with eyes twisted like a crazy vato.

"Guys," Pepe said, stepping in, "there's no fighting allowed."

Cesar looked at Pepe, thankful he'd intervened. The three to one odds didn't favor Cesar. He left the living room red-faced, and walked outside to the patio. He heard laughing as he walked away. I can't let those guys laugh at me, he thought. Should I go back and confront them? Cesar decided he'd be better off smoking a cigarette.

In 2008 when Pepe was seven, his dad, Rafael, bought a house in a middle-class Juarez neighborhood. Rafael converted the home to an installation for the addicted and their visiting family members, and named it, Nueva Vida. He had been involved in the venture at first, but found a good set of counselors could manage the site. He allowed Pepe to hang around Nueva Vida. For patients with children, Pepe was a reminder, a motivation for them to get sober. Pepe also provided much needed levity and unwavering support.

Cesar's cigarette smoke didn't offend Pepe in the least. At Nueva Vida, patients and visitors smoked freely, so Pepe was used to the smell of burning tobacco.

"What do you want?" Cesar asked.

"Whatcha up to?" Pepe asked.

"Smoking a cigarette. Can't you see, chingado?"

"I'm glad you didn't die," he said, sitting on a metal chair, one of the chairs that were used for group sessions in the evenings. It was the beginning of summer in Ciudad Juarez. The temperature was around ninety degrees. Corrugated metal sheets, on top of wooden columns and parallel beams, protected the patio from the oppressive rays of the sun. "I would've missed you."

"Why?" Cesar asked. It was the first time anyone had said that to him.

"You're smart. You fixed Carmen's computer; got rid of all those viruses. Plus I like that you say 'chingado' all the time."

"You like that, you little chingado?" Cesar asked, flicking the cigarette butt across the patio toward the dirt backyard.

Pepe fell to the floor and grabbed his gut, laughing hysterically at Cesar's witty response. Cesar, hardcore as he was, couldn't help cracking a smile.

Cesar hated personal counseling sessions with Felipe. Because Carmen was a woman, he ignored and was often rude to her. Felipe was a macho like him, and he didn't take Cesar's shit.

"Fifteen minutes outside is all you get," Felipe said to Cesar, during their one-on-one time.

"That's bullshit! That's barely enough time for me to go across the street and back."

"If you don't like it—"

"I know," Cesar said, cutting him off, "I can leave for good." He got up upset from his chair and walked quickly toward the door.

"Group session is in twenty minutes!"

Cesar headed for his shared room, with a full head of steam. I don't need this place, he said to himself, beginning to gather his things. Roberto, a forty-year-old man, sat upright on his own bed, smoking a cigarette, and reading the newspaper. The room was shared by four patients. Roberto was the resident veteran, "the most experienced of all," he told the others one day, on account of all of the mistakes he'd made in his life.

"You don't want to do that," he said.

"Do what?" Cesar asked, abruptly.

"Leave this place."

"Who asked you?" Cesar asked, looking around the room, struggling to gather his things. "Just give me a cigarette and keep your mouth shut, old man."

"Sorry," Roberto said, "this is my last one."

Cesar pulled a gym bag from underneath his bed. He placed all of his items in the bag, and stormed out of the room, needing a cigarette (laced with heroin if possible) really bad.

"I'm out of this dump," he said, taking one final look, seeing Roberto bury his head in the newspaper.

"Cesar, where ya going?" Pepe asked, catching a glimpse of Cesar heading out to the street.

"None of your business, you little chingado," he said, stepping outside. The sun's glare temporarily blinded him. He stopped, allowing his eyes to adjust. Pepe caught up.

"You're not leaving us, are you?" Pepe asked.

"What gave it away?" he asked, sarcastically. "The bag?" He paced back and forth in front of the house.

He looks like a fire ant after I poke it with a stick, Pepe said to himself. Pepe had witnessed the suffering of many patients during their withdrawal bouts. He knew the symptoms.

"¡Tranquilízate, Cesar! (Calm yourself, Cesar!)," he said, but his plea came too late.

Cesar bent over, hacking, grabbing his convulsing stomach. A projectile of vomit came out of his mouth. After dry heaving a couple of times, Cesar stood-up, hands behind his neck like a criminal about to be arrested, and took a deep breath.

"You alright?" Pepe asked.

"You ask some pretty stupid questions sometimes," Cesar said, wiping his mouth with the bottom of his T-shirt.

"Yeah, I know. Sorry. Hey, I know what you need. Follow me!"

Pepe led Cesar across the street to the general store. "You need a beer, but not a 40-ouncer, okay?" Pepe asked, rhetorically. "Just a 12oz can. Don't drink all of it either—" he said, following him to the refrigerator—"just half. It'll help with your symptoms until you get medication again from the doctor."

They walked to the cash register. Cesar waited in line. Pepe went over to the side, pulling a comic from a stand, and began flipping its pages.

"What are you doing?" Cesar asked, noticing Pepe scanning the comic book.

"Looking at the pictures."

"You're not going to read it?"

"No," he said, "I don't know how to read, so I just look at the funny drawings."

Because Cesar was broke, Pepe had to buy the beer. They walked back to Nueva Vida.

"How come you can't read?" Cesar asked.

"The specialist said I have a learning disability. And something called 'dyslexia.'"

Frustrated with his son's performance, and tired of listening to his son complain, Pepe's father allowed him to stop attending school in 3rd grade. "You can be of use to me at the center," he said to Pepe. "You won't need reading there."

A few days later, it occurred to Cesar that he could teach Pepe to read.

Perhaps Cesar felt obliged to help because Pepe had helped him? Perhaps Cesar was a nice guy, with a soft heart for children in need of assistance?

"Come outside with me, chingado," he told Pepe, taking some of Roberto's old newspapers from a pile. They sat side-by-side on the patio. Pepe sat quietly. "What's this letter here?" he said, pointing at a capitalized "A" in the newspaper.

"Uh, I don't know."

"Okay," Cesar said, "don't worry. We'll start from the beginning."

Unlike school teachers, who were restricted by the need to help other students, Cesar could focus on Pepe. Day after day, he had Pepe work with him, despite Pepe's stalling. "I think Carmen's calling me," Pepe said once during a session. "I don't hear anything," Cesar said. "Can I go to the bathroom?" Pepe asked Cesar all the time.

Cesar had him circle every "a" he could find in a paragraph, then the "e's," until Pepe could identify all of the vowels and sound them out. Once Pepe mastered the vowels, Cesar repeated his instructional technique with the consonants.

Carmen was pleasantly surprised by Cesar's commitment and passion. As a counselor, she understood the effects of positive reinforcement. "You're doing an excellent job with Pepe," she said to him one day. "Oh, and 'Scarface' doesn't suit you anymore. From now on, I'm calling you, el Profe (the Professor)."

Cesar's pedagogy was unconventional, but it worked. While teaching Pepe, Cesar learned many things about himself. With a purpose, he could be patient, and stay still for once. He was capable of trusting another person. Indirectly, Pepe helped Cesar kick his drug habit. Cesar didn't have time to obsess about drugs, with his mind constantly thinking of what literature to use, or what words to introduce as new vocabulary. Cesar overheard Puppet and the other malandros at Nueva Vida call him, "soft." Whatever, he thought. I know I'm not 'soft.'

During hot summer days, residents of Ciudad Juarez take refuge from the heat in their homes. Right about noon, they turned on their oscillating fans, or air conditioners, if they could afford them. After la comida, or late lunch, they take a power siesta. A siesta renews everyone's alertness and strength to finish the day. Trying to do anything else is hellish. Ciudad Juarez was scorching. The temperature was 113 degrees Fahrenheit.

Walking out of Nueva Vida, Cesar felt like he'd been pressed by a hot iron. He'd run out of cigarettes, and midday was as good as any other time to go across the street. As much as he tried, he couldn't fall asleep during the day.

Cesar crossed the street. The neighborhood looked deserted. Cesar stepped inside the general store. The owner was sitting behind the cash register. A wood panel about three inches thick, carved with names and tag monikers, served as his countertop. He looks miserable, Cesar thought, getting a closer look at the man. The man's face was pale and clammy, with sweat falling below his sideburns. A little oscillating fan, set on high, hung on a wall to the owner's left.

"Can I help you?" he said, staring at Cesar with a look of repulsion. I wish this center for lowlifes would close down, he thought.

"Some Fiesta cigarettes," he said. Fuck-you too, old man, Cesar thought.

The man turned around. He reached for a carton of Fiesta cigarettes that was inside a top cabinet. He struggled, trying to pull out a single pack. To pass the time, Cesar looked at magazine covers displayed on a stand to his left. He saw Pepe's comic book; the one he saw Pepe select from the stand as an illiterate boy. Over two months had gone by since that day, and since the day of Cesar's overdose. Through it all, Cesar had stayed sober.

The store owner placed the pack on the countertop.

"That'll be seventy-five pesos," he said.

"Oh, and this comic book also." Cesar and Pepe had made substantial progress. Pepe was now reading short sentences. This will be perfect, Cesar thought, holding the comic in front of him with both hands. Pepe will finally get to see what he's been missing.

Cesar headed for the store exit. He pushed the door open, getting blinded by the sun. To avoid having to squint, he put his head down. He held the comic book in front of him again, flipping the cover, and beginning to reading. He walked onto the sidewalk. The street was empty and silent. Cesar's chuckles echoed along the boulevard. A few steps from the center, half-way across the street, Cesar was startled by loud noises: Clunk! Clunk!

Cesar took his eyes off the comic book, recognizing the sound of car doors being slammed. Staring at Cesar from outside their sport utility vehicles was a group of masked men, with cuernos de chivo (AK-

47's) hanging from their shoulders. Cesar's heart jumped, beating faster than it ever had.

"That's one of them!" the leader said. "¡Mátenlo!"

One of the masked men grabbed a .45 caliber Glock from his belt line. Cesar's pupils dilated and blood rushed to his legs. He was in full flight before the assassin could level his pistol. He sprinted past the general store, clutching Pepe's comic book like a track and field baton. The shop was a death trap; it had no back door. The end of the street block was Cesar's best option. Running for his life, Cesar desperately hoped he could corner the block, and be out of sight before the killer took his shot. Bang!

Over an hour later:

"What do we have here, Ortiz?" Martinez, the lead Investigator, asked a portly Officer standing in front of Nueva Vida.

"Multiple homicide scene, Sir," he said. "The proprietor is inside with his son."

"How many?"

"Well, Sir—"he said, wiping his sweaty brow with a white handkerchief. The temperature had dropped to 100 degrees—"there's twelve inside the house, including the owner's son. They were all killed execution style. The owner has identified one of them, a female, as his counselor, and the ten others were patients he said. Oh, and there's one over there." Ortiz pointed behind Martinez, to a corpse that laid face down near the street corner.

Martinez walked slowly toward Cesar's body. He stared at the corpse, examining entry wounds with scientific eyes. One shot to the back, he said to himself. He crouched. With a couple of fingers, he positioned the back of Cesar's head directly below his gaze. And there's the love tap, he thought, seeing a gaping hole in the skull. He scanned around the body for evidence. A few feet away, he noticed something on the floor. He stood, walked toward the object, and picked it up. It was Pepe's comic.

Ortiz heard Martinez chuckling, walking back to the scene of the crime.

"What do you have there, Sir?" Ortiz asked.

"It's a comic book."

"Want to go inside now, Sir?"

"Why?" Martinez asked, laughing, with his eyes on the page. "We got a recovering Telenovela star in there or something?"

"Nah," Ortiz said, "just a bunch of filthy malandros."

About C. Osvaldo Gómez

"I'm currently a High School Assistant Principal by day and a novice fiction writer by night. I broke through this year, 2011, with my first publication, "The Curb," winning first place for the month of August at WritersType.com."

Trailhead

by Jennifer Peckinpaugh

A sinister event has transpired: I lost my best girl in Witchduck— a muddy, bare spot mining town south of Momaw Lake. She was not truly lost, but taken. I swear to find the four-legged fiend who did it, but I will not make haste: only a patient wolfer gets his prey.

I cupped my hands around my mouth and called for her. The stiff whistle of an arctic wind and the call of a sharp-shinned hawk were the only replies.

"Tohami!" I shouted to my Dakota scout, panicked. "She is lost! Would she run away?"

"She was led astray. You know this; the moon was full, one track turned to many pairs of tracks, even over the howl of the storm, the cries of the pack stung your ears," Tohami replied.

"A loyal, truer companion I have never known—a ten-year-old dog in a storm like the one of two nights ago...she bravely sacrificed herself for our benefit. Do you not believe it to be true?" Scanning his eyes desperately for the answer, I could not face him as he spoke.

"You speak for Molly, but what of your heart? Your head will not accept it. Patience will reveal the truth you escape, the truth you let run amok."

Tohami spoke his perfect white English, and he did not simply speak it, but bravely delivered it as a chieftain delivers his war cry. Exhausted, he slung a rack of pelts over his shoulder, readying them for tanning.

"How much do you think you will get for the furs?" I inquired, pacing about as helplessly as a child, wanting to help, but being only competent enough to watch.

The sharp edge of the skinning stone zipped back and forth, but he did not look in my eyes. "Whatever it is, it will not be enough. The white fur traders in Mendota, they do not deal fairly with the Mdewakanton tribesmen. They believe we cannot be trusted, despite our allegiance to the treaties." He punctuated his sentence with contempt, angrily plunging the skins in boiling water.

Through a series of treaties with the United States government, he and his tribesmen had lost their land, their home. He became my brother, my fellow rambler across the earth. Although I suspect we were rightly the same age, in many ways, Tohami had become my father.

"Angus Mangoravitch, my work is hard. Tell me one of the stories of your life as a noble child—the one about your father—and the wolves."

I shook my head and watched him. Tohami stopped and dug my gaze up from under my hat. "The story is sad, but it will help take your mind away from Molly." Tohami persuaded.

"Desperate times make men do desperate, unordinary things. If he were living, my father, God rest his soul, he would surely not hear of the lot I've chosen in life." I began the story in my usual way, stoking the smoldering embers of the fire with my walking stick.

Looking down at my raw, parched hands, I remembered how my father's hands never looked like anything except fine tanned leather. "My father was a well educated Russian man—a desperate well educated Russian man. Under Tsar Alexander II, he rose to substantial local power as a wealthy land owner, and a member of the regional Duma. After his marriage to my mother, Theresa Lily Malloy, daughter of a wealthy Irish manufacturing magnate, Tsar Alexander dedicated my father to a provincial governor's post. Soon thereafter, revolutionaries assassinated the tsar. His son, Alexander III, began his ascent to power and instead of stripping my father of his power, saw his political fortitude and influence among the peasants, which my father parlayed into a position as land captain of Siberia."

Tohami stopped to rest, surveying me. "You are proud of your father."

"Of course I was. He had substantial power, but it was often unappreciated."

"Ah!" Tohami exclaimed. "Now, we come to the reason for tears."

"My father laughed when he recounted how my mother cried for a month of Sundays after learning of his Siberian transfer. All she had known was emerald green lands and sapphire blue sky and sea. Siberia was void of color, the occasional grey snow-spitting clouds being the solitary exception."

I stopped and looked up to the sky, recollecting the rolling shades of grey from my childhood. "My fondest memory, which includes a rare smile from my mother, is of walking to the home of the schoolmaster three days a week during the summer, and going with my father to inspect the progress of the Trans-Siberian Railway. Progressing from boy to man, I watched peasants, criminals and military conscripts topple massive sugar pines and strong arm steel to ground whilst negotiating icy Lake Baikal. Lurking in the late afternoons were the ever present, mysterious protectors of the railroad—volk cheloviek. When I innocently asked my father why I never saw the wolf men— wolfers— catching wolves, he gazed longingly to the lavender frosted moon, smiling, but never answered. The summer of my seventeenth year, the isolation, the severe weather, and lack of social opportunities corroded my parents' marriage. My mother left my father for a Moscow-born, Londoner. He never saw her again. In his desperation, we left Russia for Alaska—the gold rush—though I never left my memories of the wolfers. Father thought if he could get rich enough he might win her back. He perished trying...and I nearly met with the same fate snaking my way out of that God-forsaken ice box." A winter gust whipped across my face, taking my breath away, and in its place a frenzied bitterness stirred in my soul. Tohami never looked up from his work.

Surveying the confluence of the Mississippi and the Missouri Rivers, I crawled into our makeshift shelter—an outcropping nestled at the foot of the Misquah Hills. I waited for Tohami's footsteps behind me, but they did not follow. Growing impatient, I skipped a rock across the lake, hoping to drive him from his thought.

"Look into your heart, and you will know it is true, Angus Mangoravitch."

"It's Malloy, you dunce!" Irritated, I shouted back. "My father took my mother's last name after we arrived in Alaska so we wouldn't look like a couple of dense foreigners seeking our fortune."

"You stray in your thoughts. Rekindling the past does not spark the future."

Quickly, I crawled on all fours out of the outcropping and hotly whirled around to confront his calm gaze. "You think the wolves took my girl, took my best wolfing pup, thieved my Molly?"

"Yes. And do you not agree?"

I rubbed the flat, smooth lapis stone in my pocket, the intense blue color that reminded me of my mother's eyes. She had found it on the shore of Lake Baikal the summer she left me; it was the only thing I had left of her, save a few errant memories.

"Yes, Molly is too loyal a dog to up and leave. She surely was taken off. And now what shall become of us my wise friend, with no one to lead us? "

"I lead myself," Tohami volleyed his answer back to me. "And why is that not true for you?"

We hadn't seen the sun for nearly a week when we stepped foot into the Minnesota Territory, an untamed, disorderly land full of promise for prospectors, empire builders, free men of color and the like. In a tumble-down hobo camp, we hunkered down for what the locals called the May Grays. Trekking from Siberia, and then Alaska, I hadn't the heart to tell them all how exquisitely miserable spring could actually be. In keeping my ear to the ground, word spread like wildfire of jobs—good jobs, too. The American Fur Company posted signs from Fort Frances, Ontario to Mendota, Minnesota Territory, advertising for trappers, skinners, and outpost men. And any variety of logging companies would hire, but I set my sights on the steaming metal beast of my childhood: the railroad.

The Hill and Company Employment Outpost consisted of nothing more than a ramshackle canvas tent with one measly oil lamp for light. The frigid early morning gusts pulled apart the corner edges of the tent like a delicate flower. If I had had a stick I could not have stirred the men—a stew of all ages, all nationalities, from every walk of life.

"Got a name, young man?" A wiry grey haired man licked his thumbs and handed me a pencil and a piece of paper, and motioning to them, asked, "You can read and write?"

"Yes, of course I can."

He waved his hand, dismissing my answer. "Well, I gotta ask. There's so many who can't. Now, what was the name again?"

"Malloy. Angus Malloy."

"You got any experience wolfing, Mr. Malloy?"

My father had been an honorable man, so much so that I had found it difficult, but not impossible, to master the art of lying. "Yes, sir, I just came off a job in Alaska, wolfing for a mining operation out of Sitka, and before that for the Trans-Siberian Railroad—Lake Baikal region. I've got good experience; I'm patient." I stood confidently with my hands in my pockets, rocking back and forth on my heels. He didn't seem impressed or swayed one way or the other.

"You got a good wolfing dog? And I don't mean no pup—a solid set of eyes to guard your back. Them beasts is thick up in the woods." He cast his pencil up past my nose, toward the evergreen ocean. "You don't want to be there after dark—alone." He stroked his wiry black beard, as if only he knew the mysteries of the woods. He shrugged his chin toward Tohami. "That your Injun friend there?"

I nodded.

"His kind ain't welcome to apply here. The fur traders, they like them."

"I...my dog...she ran off. I aim to find her, but...Tohami is my other set of eyes. He's better than a dog." Earnestly, I watched his eyes scour Tohami.

"We pay for one, not both. And don't be coming back later saying different. You seem like a fine young man, perfectly capable, and you certainly have the experience. I'll take you and your Injun friend, but the first sign of trouble out of either one of you, and you're gone! Come back tonight—dusk. Don't be late, neither!"

Moonlight cast a soft glow on the vast spread of lifeless branches that towered over me. In the distance, a wagon, drawn by two massive Belgians, waited for its work crew, heralding the end of the shift for day-tripper types who show up to finish the shifts of the infirmed. But for a handful of us, those who choose to toil in the murky shadows of the pines and the maples and the mountains, this is our lot. Listening to the snorts and whinnies of the Belgians, I could only make out their sparse outlines puffing wispy trails of warm breath. Molly rolled about in my mind, and I thought about the day she disappeared. A pack of wolves had been trailing our heels since Fort Frances. To keep them at bay, I employed a trick of the Chinese wolfers—firecrackers. Scared the wits out of the beasts! Of course, it was no acceptable replacement for an experienced pup, as firecrackers could sometimes disrupt even the gentle, unwavering nature of the Belgians and the Clydesdales. Scampering off, I watched her forge ahead to find water. She was not to be found. Tohami and I searched lakeside, in outcroppings, caves, mine shafts, all of Witchduck proper, and...my heart barely limped its beat. My father had adopted Molly—a Chuksha—after my mother had left us, and she was as much a mother to me as my bored, desperate mother had ever been. From across Momaw Lake, the wolf howls taunted us; when in a pack, they harmonize, rather than chorus on one note, creating the illusion of there being more wolves than there actually are. I suspected that they were hunkered down in one of the outcroppings on the lake, keeping sentinel on the twinkling embers of our fire. Wolves will often set up ambushes near water holes, often using the same site repeatedly. Despite the biting beads of ice and snow that pelted us, I insisted upon sending Molly scouting for water. I listened as the wolf calls changed. When pursuing prey, they emit higher pitched howls, concentrating on two notes. Soon, the howls metamorphosed into long, smooth sounds—the sounds used for calling pack mates to a kill.

"Mr. Malloy! Good to see you. One of the few who actually show up—nice clear night, it'll be a cold one."

"Not as cold as it could be, sir." Turning on my heels, the wiry grey haired man with the wiry black beard from the jobs office strode heavily on the frozen mud, cricking and cracking in time with his warning.

"Ah! That's always the case." He shoved his hands into his coat pockets. "So, where's your Injun friend? Decided it was too cold for him?"

"A Dakota keeps his word. No matter what our Great Spirit Father sends to us—rain, snow, wind, cold, drought—the Dakota keep a promise honorable." Draped in a fine beaver pelt, Tohami marched out of the shadows of the pines and stood in silence.

"Well, then," the jobs man continued, "let's not make haste. There are things to be done. Haul your sorry backsides into the wagon." With the little wiry haired man commanding the reigns, Tohami and I rode only with the sound of the Belgians lightly straining to pull the wagon deeper into the forest shroud.

"This here," the little man continued, pointing in the direction of the Saint Anthony Falls, "will be the beginning of one of the most successful, privately funded railroads in the history of our existence. That is, if you fellas can keep the wolves and the damn Indians from ruining it."

Ahead of us, the sound of the rushing of water over rock beckoned Tohami to motion to the falls. "Our god of water, Oanktehi, who lives beneath the falling water, teaches the Dakota to spread gentle peace. But your people, the whites, ignoring treaties and contracts, stole and raped our land, leaving nothing for our people to eat...and a very few angry, hungry Dakota kill whites because of their frustration. The killings were not right, and now, the whites claim we are enemies. As a child, my grandfather taught us of the story of a powerful warrior's wife who killed herself and their two children by leaping into these falls, in anguish and forlorn love for the husband who had assumed a second wife. My blood family is Dakota, but I have taken a second brother with the whites, despite the flaws with your kind. I would only request that you offer me the same consideration."

The hoof trots of the Belgians were the only sounds that passed between us until we broke through the base and supply camp clearing. Towering piles of massive pine logs neighbored row after row of moonlight-gleaming steel, flanked by heaps of picks, shovels, Fresno scrapers, hammers, spikes, and a dozen dump carts. A gaping chow house door prompted the little wiry haired man to furiously jump from the wagon cursing to blue blazes. Pointing to the door, he slammed it shut, lecturing, "No accounts don't have 'nough sense to keep the damn door closed! Where do they think food comes from? I'll be glad we get you wolfers up here; help me keep the loose ends tied up." In the distance, I heard a pack of howls, deep in the woods. With an awful chill creeping up my back, I felt Tohami's eyes on me; he knew the wolves would soon come out, searching to make an easy meal out of the chow house.

"Tohami, why don't you survey outside the perimeter of the camp and I will take the inside perimeter, including the buildings. We need to be certain the main area is secure." The wiry haired man and I took a tedious promenade through camp, checking every nook, cranny and hollow place where any variety of critter could exist; a lone opossum and a darling raccoon pair were turned out, but no wolves—or their pups—were found. Climbing back up into the wagon, I stood on the bench seat, surveying the entire area, when a long black wire caught by a gust of wind snared my attention.

"What is this wire?" I pointed as far as my eyes could see in both directions. "Are these new explosives?"

The wiry haired man shook his head and scowled. "Nah! That's a telegraph wire! I done told you this is going to be one of the most successful railroad projects that ever was. Mr. James Hill, the tycoon who's financing this little project, decided that while he's clearing and improving the area, there's no harm in putting in telegraph lines." Proudly shoving his ruddy hands in his vest, he conjectured, "Minnesota will be the envy of all the states soon enough." He spit square on the ground to seal the proclamation.

"Angus!" I whirled around to meet the fearful eyes of Tohami. He had discovered something. "In the perimeter between the camp and the cliffs of the falls, there are many dead animals—too many. The denning season is still upon us, and the wolf pups are learning to hunt. Frozen, half-eaten carcasses litter ice-topped sections of the river, some miles below the falls. Adult wolves have driven prey onto the crusted ice, ravines, and steep banks to slow them, allowing the pups a chance to make a kill. This pack has exceptional hunters."

The wiry haired man snorted, remarking, "Just kill 'em then! You ain't heard it from me, but now many a wolfer has seen his fortune in selling wolf pelts for a lot of money—a lot. Of course, anything you can do so that I can keep that our secret would be much obliged." He thumbed his hairy nose, sneering at Tohami.

On the seventeenth of May, one final frost scattered itself across the mountain tops, sugaring roof tops and tender new leaves that had only just sprouted. Tohami and I had heard the wolf pups, but had not yet caught sight of them, except for one brave soul. His front side crouched under the backside of the chow house, devouring some undesirable item. I poked him in the hind shanks and he quickly burrowed out, meeting my blue eyes with only childlike surprise. By now, all of the pups would be knee high, and full of foolish aggression, but still frightened by the sight of man, by our violent stench, our sounds, and our ways. During these times at night, I understand the wolf. His actions reflect his true nature—cunning, loving, vicious, cruel. He does not—he cannot—allow his circumstances to impede his survival. As he is true to his nature, I am an imitator.

"Your thoughts stray again?" Tohami said aloud, not so much asking me as he was explaining my silence to the wolves around us. "Angus Mangoravitch, you spend much time entertaining the past. Do you never consider the future?" Tohami punctuated the end of his sentence with a grunt as he whittled off the end of a maple branch.

My branch was not so cleanly honed; instead it stuck awkwardly bowed with a roughly chiseled point. I swung it in Tohami's direction. "Of course I consider the future! I have no aspirations of making a living in this manner; I can imagine a nice plat of land, a solid house I built with these two hands, and a soft, warm, beautiful woman who will bear my sons....Someday, not now, but someday." Resting my head in my hands, I traced the stars of Virgo, recollecting the story of Persephone who was trapped in hell with Hades for half of the year, and her forlorn mother who kept the stars in the sky as a way to remember her daughter until her return. The winters in Siberia felt much like a prison sentence, until spring returned and we celebrated Maslenitsa—the end of winter party, the week before Lent. My mother fattened my belly with thick milk, exquisitely dyed eggs, almost too lovely to eat, with briny sausages and cheese—all forbidden during Lent. Our music, games, and masquerade parties paid no attention to the rising and setting of the sun.

Tohami crouched beside me and pointed, interrupting my childhood reverie. "There, on the bluff, he is the one, the leader of the pack."

The stunning creature turned directly to face us, with a slow, deliberate movement. Standing high, hackles raised, he called once. Immediately, a smaller, yet, equally dominate wolf appeared at his side.

"She is his helpmate."

"She is his life mate," Tohami added. Dissonant chords echoed across the valley; they were calling their pack.

"They are coming, and they are seeking food, and perhaps, something else," Tohami warned, sharply gazing at me. "You must be strong and cunning, like the wolf. He is the warrior without weakness, without vulnerability. You must hone in on the present, and do not consider your action in the past. Molly is gone, as is your mother. You must let them have peace in your heart if you are to face your future."

"This job has nothing to do with my mother, or with Molly!" I countered, beating his comment back with my voice.

Tohami shook his head and continued to grind the charcoal for his face paint. "My friend, no event in life leaves us unaltered. Look at the sky, simply enough! When it snows, we become cold. When we are chased by a bear, we become frightened of the bear. And so it continues. You were abandoned, not once, but twice—and you were altered. You do not follow in your father's steps because they seem too large; you do not follow your mother because she left no trail; you do not follow Molly because you refuse to understand the story on the trail. Your spirit is in limbo; you live your life during the night, and at daybreak you retreat into your sarcophagus of memories. This is not living! Find the wolf who took Molly, and find some light for your soul, my friend. This is what men do." Tohami smeared a thick daub of black charcoal paste on his face, and did the same for me. The little wiry haired man had left me with a Remington single-shot rim fire rifle, which I loaded surreptitiously. One familiar sound from my rifle, and the pack would scatter. Tohami and I waited while a thick velvet cloud rolled in to shroud the mountain tops. Besides a careful set of eyes, patience is the wolfer's best asset.

The desolate glow of early-morning embers woke me; the warmth of the night fire had lulled Tohami and me into slumber. Yet despite the smoldering fire's heat, I felt chilled, and incredibly frightened. At my feet, the alpha male stood; his body, ears and tail low, fur sleek. On my back, I was completely vulnerable, yet his body signs showed submission. His massive paws were matted with tiny balls of mud and ice; he stepped closer and curiously sniffed me, keeping his dark eyes stationed on me.

"Are you the one? Did you take my Molly?" I whispered. He lowered his head, pausing before he moved his snout up my leg. Tohami lay motionless, unaware. Holding out my palm, I tossed him the last bit of my supper—roasted rabbit. He sniffed and gobbled it up in one bite. Tohami jumped up at the sound of cracking wood, a patch being peeled from the back of the chow house. A pack—10 to 15— banded around two young males, bent on destroying the building and gaining access. The alpha male quickly looked over his back and beared his teeth at me in a wicked grin, a growl traveling from low in his throat. His friendly ruse goaded me to anger.

"Judas! Bastard traitor! You come back I swear I will kill you!" Reaching to my side, I grabbed for the Remington, but without conviction. I fired two warning shots into the air. I did not wish to kill such a noble, cunning creature, but for Molly, for me...the beast leapt over the fire and lead his pack, hugger-mugger toward the safety of the den.

Waving his hands above his head and cursing in his native Dakota, Tohami looked back over his shoulder, waiting for me to approach the wolves, to finish them off. I did not. The truth of the matter is that I wished for them to return, hoping to see all the members of the pack, especially the young females.

Tohami looked to the dawn breaking through the cloudy sky, but would not look to me until after the sun had made its full ascent over the mountain top. "For many, last night would have been the end to your time on earth. You were spared, for a reason." He slowly sipped on his chicory coffee, pondering the reasons. "Perhaps you are a spirit."

I nervously laughed, explaining, "People have spent a great deal of time telling me what I was not—not Russian nobility like my father, not a miner, not an industrialist, not even my own man, either—so much so that I have forgotten what exactly it is that I am." With my palms to the fire, I touched the spot where the male wolf had brushed against me.

"No one has said you are not a hunter, a wolfer? No one tells the bear he is a bear. No one tells the wind how to blow. The spirits have decided your destiny. And you, my friend, are without recourse."

"Am I? Or am I without hope?"

He laughed, wagging his finger at me. "Ah! Look to your white man's religion for your answer, but I think there is always hope because there is no escaping your fate. You and your wolf—twisted inside out—you exist in his skin and him in yours. Fate is a fickle mistress and she is calling. Will you answer?"

When the wiry haired man saw the hole in the back of the chow house, his face went red while he stomped and cursed; purple veins popped to the top of the skin on his neck.

"Mr. Hill ain't paying you to let the wolves run amok! Men say they heard shots last night. You hit the bastard?" With his hand on his hip, he impatiently lingered in his stomped spot of melting snow.

I shook my head. "It was dark, and there were many—15 or 20. Sorry, sir. It will not happen again."

"Dern right it won't! If it does, you can pack your bags and hit the trail!" His abrupt about-face startled me. "You got a telegraph message down at the bottom of the mountain. Better hoof it there—might be important."

The telegraph office at the bottom of the mountain resembled a fairy tale house in the woods. The creak of an opening door announced my arrival.

"Ah! Irish eyes are smiling, my boy!" A dwarfish man—wire-rimmed glasses, beady eyes, gimp—tottered toward the desk with a crisp, yellow square of paper in hand.

"You Angus Malloy?"

"Yes, sir, I am."

"Your telegraph came all the way from the emerald isle! Exciting! It's our first up here on this mountain, except for the official ones from Mr. Hill, of course." Pushing it under my nose, he pushed up his glasses and motioned for me to read it. "Must be some fancy, rich bugger who bothers to send one of these...you ain't curious who sent it?" He tried to peer up under the brim of my hat, but I did not need to see the sender, or even the message. There was only one woman who could have summoned the gods the way she surely did to find me.

"Thank you, sir." I tipped my hat and scattered back up the mountain.

"You are very silent this evening. I sense something is troubling you. Perhaps it is a woman?" Tohami and I pushed around the grub in our bowls; the table was empty, except for us two—a winter tinged draft had evacuated the entire back corner of the chow house.

"My mother is coming to visit me—tomorrow."

"It has been a long time since you've seen her."

"Yes," I sighed, remembering her forced smile and sad blue eyes, "nearly ten years ago."

Tohami rested his chin on the plateau of his folded hands. "What will you do?"

"I do not know. I could refuse to see her, send her away; however...one should not send one's mother away. Yet, I owe her nothing."

Tohami smiled, "Except life, of course." He continued, "Will you never release your bitterness?"

"And what if I do not?" I answered, angrily letting my spoon fall into my bowl.

"You did not see her leave, without so much as a glance backwards, and watch as my father worked himself into an old, embittered man—he died of a broken heart! And he was not the only one; she wounded my heart, too. This nomad's life of mine has been as much about escaping old memories as it has been about chasing my vocation."

"Your heart has healed, but it is still tender. You are frightened of her arrival?"

"I am frightened of having my heart broken again, my friend."

The shrill shift change whistle called us to the cold, dark forest. Tohami and I settled under an enormous, fragrant pine tree, waiting for the sun to pitch its last aureate spokes and retreat behind the mountains. I wondered if we would see the wolves, and whether my mother would truly be in my sights the next morning. Against the canvas of a disappearing horizon, these questions and theories tumbled to and fro in my mind. Having not the energy for answers, I crawled to my station and waited.

Between my third empty cup of coffee and the low, warm midnight glow of Tohami's fire, I heard the wolf pack call. Impossible to tell how many or how far away they were, I summoned Tohami with the shriek of a hungry great horned owlet. His response, an adult-to-owlet distress call, drove my clenched hands tighter to the Remington. With most of the snow having already melted, a flash of white snared my attention. From under a pin cherry thicket, a fluff of white wriggled toward me—Molly. The animal looked identical to Molly—a white and blonde chuksha with piebald spotting. She softly, shyly trod to me, and I stood. Holding out my hand, she licked it.

"Molly! How I have worried myself sick over you! What has come of you?" Vigorously, I brushed her fur with my hand, pushing my nose against her muzzle and her fur, then noticed her frame was meatier than I had remembered. She reluctantly gazed at me, both brown eyes showing a skittish nature that I did not recall in her temperament. Molly had been born with one brown eye and one that was parti-colored—blue with brown streaks. Had it changed or was this my foolish, wishful imagination playing tricks on me? In a panic, I grabbed her around the neck, turning her eyes toward me and was toppled to the ground by a large male wolf. Quickly, I rolled to my right and fumbled along the ground until I felt the butt of the Remington. With a backward side-step snarl, the male leapt over the thicket; Molly disappeared.

"Molly! Molly! Molly!" I forlornly screeched it at the top of my lungs. The forest's perfect silence was the sole response. I shot three times into the air. My breathy rage answered back. From the corner of my eye, Tohami quietly approached me and put his hand on my shoulder.

"You are not well, my friend." He felt my cheek and my neck. "You are fevered. It is probably the catarrh. I will prepare a dogwood and sassafras tea. Be still and rest." He laid his hands on me and quickly left. I whispered softly for Molly, my mind wrestling between the vision of what I had seen and what I instinctively knew to be true: Molly had left me, and whether alive or dead, she would not be coming back.

Images of this ghost dog taunted me during the night, frightfully pulling me from a deep slumber, despite Tohami's prayerful vigil.

Morning greeted me in the shoulder blades—the toe of the wiry haired man's boot.

"You gonna just lay there? You got some fine company up there at the top of that mountain." He lustfully looked toward the summit, placing his hat over his heart. "I'd get up there if I were you. Don't want to keep a woman like that waiting—she might leave or worse—might get taken!" He snickered and tromped further down the hill with his coffee, scratching his day-old whiskers.

Dawn rose over the mountain that morning earlier than usual—spring. An air of hope and good cheer threaded its way among the men. They laughed and japed about with each other in a fresh, pleasant way, unusual for the dead of winter. My fever and confusion had lifted as fog does with the dawn; it mattered not whether the wolf had been Molly or...something else. She was gone, and in the place that made her happy. In my glad observation, I was unaware of the tender hand that rested on my shoulder. Twisting my head over my shoulder, my eyes followed the gloved hand, up a thin, beautifully shrouded arm to the delicate face I had always known as Mother.

"Angus! My darling! How are you my sweet, sweet son?" Her eyes dribbled tears, and I wondered whether they were of the contrite variety or the kind women produce for convenient drama. Thinking my response should have come much more quickly than it did, she oddly cocked her head and reached out for my forehead.

"You're not well?"

I pushed her hand away—gently. "It's nothing—a fever. It comes and goes. My friend Tohami has given me medicine. In his tribe—the Dakota— he was a shaman."

And then, I saw the soured, dour face I remember of my wintry childhood. "Really, Angus, I should think that a person of your breeding could choose a more suitable companion." She neatly tugged at her gloved hands, sending polite glances to the curious onlookers.

"Well, I suppose I could have, but they've all left. When I had no one, Tohami has been a loyal friend—unfortunately, a quality frequently underrated by some." I held her icy stare until she motioned toward the mountain peak.

"Mr. Hill was nice enough to allow me use of his chalet. He's a family friend, you know."

"No, I was not aware of that. Did he know Father?"

"No, darling, he's an acquaintance of my fiancé."

"Yes, your family, not mine." I kicked a dirt clod. "Does Mr. Hill have hot running water up there?" I asked, pitching my head toward the chalet.

My mother beamed. "Why, of course dear. Will you do me the honor of being my guest? I have something I would like to give to you...something your father would be proud for you to have."

The curious glances turned to stares as Mother and I sauntered, hand in hand, to Mr. Hill's gondola. She lived a good life, and my father would be relieved to know that; he had only wanted the best for her, and she might have been able to enjoy it if she had been the content kind of woman. But, she was not. I had come to understand that it was not in her nature to be especially faithful.

"Angus, I know my departure was not carried out in the kindest of ways, nor with the greatest of care, the way it should have been done...but you have never left my soul. I have carried your sweet face and keen nature with me. Angus! Please do not make me beg for your forgiveness! However, if it requires my wretched, pitiful tears to beseech your forgiveness, then I implore you to give me the opportunity to fall back into your good graces."

I knew she had not only come to ask my forgiveness; her contrition surely would not have held out for this long. She had come to ask forgiveness for something that, in her mind, she thought I would consider much worse than her departure so many long years ago. Mother dabbed her eyes and threw open the doors to the chalet.

Spying a settee, I collapsed into a heap, my hands covering my eyes. Cold, tired and confused, I inquired, "Are you asking my permission to get married again? Are you convinced that it's finally been long enough for all of your high society acquaintances to accept the marriage as decent?"

"Angus, darling, it is not my friends, nor my acquaintances, nor even my family. I want to know, I must know that you are happy and at peace with your life. That is all I have ever wanted for you."

"And what did you think I wanted when you left me, no more than an oversized child?" I shouted, tossing every pillow from the settee on the floor. "Did it not ever occur to you that what I really wanted, what I really needed was my mother? I did not require being dragged from pillar to post by a man too utterly despondent to take care of himself! Father died from a broken heart—and it was your doing!" I yelled through my tears, flailing my arms at her outstretched ones as she tried to bring me to her bosom for comforting, as a mother does for her child. And, I remembered, at this very moment, I was a child—her child. I lay with my head in her lap for a very long time, gazing up at her. She was still very beautiful and I understood how my father could have lost his will to keep living without her.

"Darling, won't you come back to Ireland with me? I can take care of you." She mopped my wet brow with her handkerchief. "Arthur can find a nice job for you, something in Dublin, perhaps?" I shook my head; she smiled.

"I thought as much." She playfully wrapped a piece of my hair around her finger. "You are your father's child—never one to accept any form of charity. You simply will not have it unless you've worked to earn it, meandering about from this post to that one. Nothing I can offer to change your mind?"

Before my brain could even process an answer, a screech answered in my place, and I leapt off of the settee, grabbing at the knife on my belt.

Mother laughed, which resonated throughout the room, sending the screeching into heaven's limits. "This is what I wanted to give you, what you and your father could only appreciate."

"What the hell is it?"

Mother quickly trotted across the room to a large square box, covered with heavy canvas wrap. As she placed her hands on the parcel, she turned to look over her shoulder at me, grinning as a naughty child might.

"Do you want to know how I found you?" she playfully warbled.

I shook my head. "I want to know what is under that wrap! Pull it off, please!"

"Arthur keeps impeccable records of all his endeavors—materials, equipment, manpower. He supplies Mr. Hill with much of the railroad building equipment and engineers. Every week, I poured over each ledger, praying to find your name, and I knew I would. I remember the way you and your father stood, fixed upon the railroad building at Lake Baikal. At night, I heard you ask him about those men, the ones who drove away the beasts of the night, and so, I clung to the hope that you would find your way...back to me. And, I was right. This gift—an antidote for all the poison between us."

Motioning to me, I cautiously approached the cage and taking her hand, we gently tugged at the wrap until it dropped to the floor. My legs fell out from under me and I wept as a child at the magnificent sight: berkut.

"Aquila c. chrysaetos—golden eagle—when I was a child, I heard tales of these birds, hunting and killing wolves, but I never witnessed it. The native peoples claimed the bird had mystic powers...certainly it deserves reverence."

The bird watched me with its intense eyes, slowly turning its head. Its sleek, feathered body glowed with gold on its crown and nape, and white epaulettes draped the wing tips, which faded to a strong coffee color.

"She's been trained in falconry. The golden eagles were nearly hunted to extinction—there's a significant market for their feathers, as you probably know—until our Irish government banned their destruction. On the Isle of Man, the Manx are hand raising the raptors, for repopulating Scotland and Ireland." Strumming her fingers along the cage, Mother continued, "Do you think she'll be a good hunter?"

I ignored Mother and gingerly opened the cage door. The bird gingerly lowered her head and stepped onto my arm with a sense of belonging, even entitlement. With wings spread, her shadow enveloped mine.

"What is her name?"

Mother shrugged her shoulders. "She is yours to name. I am only the messenger."

As night approached, I watched the berkut keenly, hoping an air of inspiration would gust about and I could finally give the animal a name. With lights at the base camp twinkling—disappearing and reappearing—they soon vanished as if a wet, damp cloth had snuffed them out. My berkut sat on the top of the world—her cage—and she and I spent a rare peaceful night, regarding the stars as one admires a fistful of jewels.

An abrupt blinding flash of light, followed by a ground-trembling shock jolted me to immediate alertness. I scampered to the gondola and razored down the hill. The wiry haired man stationed himself in front of the chow house, his Mississippi rifle cocked and aimed. He lowered the muzzle when he saw me; a hole the size of a ripe watermelon had been blown into the north side of the chow house.

"You! This is your damn fault!" He took long awkward strides toward me. "I shoulda known better than to hire a Russian zek! I told you if anything like this happened again..."

Interrupting, I pointed to the hole in the building. "I don't believe I had anything to do with your handiwork there." The group of men that had surrounded us snickered quietly, hands to faces; no one wanted to be on the receiving end of the wiry haired man's wrath.

"I ain't talking about that!" he bellowed. "Get down on your belly and look at what them beasts done!"

As he instructed, I touched my stomach to the dirt and saw what he had been shooting at under the chow house. "A hole—they probably tunneled in from the other side. It's not unusual for wolves to dig holes for dens, especially in colder climates. I'll fill it in and tonight, I'll be back on duty, sir. The pack will return. I have no doubt, and when they do...."

Shaking his head, he replied, "You'll do no such thing! I done told you last time was the last chance. Sorry son."

A navy hem cut a swath through the circle of men, who parted with awe at my mother, the berkut perched upon her arm.

"Sir, I believe the young man deserves another chance. After all, it was not his fault; my travel schedule interrupted his work. Please, surely a man of your stature can see the practicality of the situation. And, he's prepared to hunt now—meet Zvezda—the answer to your wolf problem." She had named the berkut the nickname my father had called her—my little star. She continued, "Only Angus can hunt her, only he understands her nature. What say you?" With a numbing stare, the little wiry haired man did the only thing he could: he bowed to us both and walked away.

"My work here is done," she purred to me.

These last words, this last expression I saw on Theresa Lily Malloy's face was a smirk. I kept vigil on her mule-drawn caravan until I could no longer see its sidestepping descent from the mountain. Silently, I stood glued in the spot from where she began her descent. From across continents and oceans, she had been with me, though not knowing my circumstances; she understood how her departure had painfully shaped me into a man. While I was not sure she felt remorse for leaving as she had, I was sure that she loved me—then and now.

As the spring staged its full assault on our mountain, the daylight began to linger, and Zvezda quickly learned her trade. Within weeks, she had wounded a dozen or more adult gray wolves and killed two wolf pups; the raids on the chow house soon became the fuel for fireside yarns spun by camp old timers. Yet, I sensed a deed undone in the wolf pack.

On the eve of the summer solstice, Tohami invited me as his guest for the tribal celebration. Clouds parted ways to welcome a blue moon. Tohami greeted me, smiling, pointing approvingly to the sky.

"Ah! My friend! You have come! Our earth mother is pleased. Did you bring Zvezda?"

Whistling, I raised my arm over my head and Zvezda glided down, settling on it.

"It has been a long time since I have seen your mother's smile on your face."

"Yes, it has been a long while. Thank you for including me this evening. It is a great honor, Tohami."

At the center of the tribe, elders were placing crushed granite into a section of a large—at least 25 feet—circle, which was divided into many sections of various sizes, each containing different materials—granite, pebbles, lava stones, and sandstone.

"What is this called?" I asked.

Tohami ruminated for a moment and thoughtfully translated from his native Dakota. "It is called a medicine wheel."

"Is someone ill?"

He grabbed his stomach and guffawed. "Oh, my friend, I forget you are not familiar with the Dakota ways. This wheel is a mirror image of the wheel in the spirit world, which illuminates our path, our way toward goodness, toward blessings and balance, toward our spiritual journey in which we find our chakra, and how all of nature around us," he spun his outstretched arms in a circle, "how it finds a place for us—no beginning, no ending—a perfect circle of life."

I paused to look at the circle and then at Zevezda. I reached up and pulled one of her tail feathers. She did not flinch, towering proudly over Tohami.

"I want to make a contribution." Holding the feather, I presented it to him in the flat of my hand. Trolling to the bottom of my pocket, I then pulled out the lapis stone. I remembered that Mother's eyes had not been the same blue—lapis blue—as I had remembered. I did not need the stone now. I had new memories of her.

"You and I—we are different, and yet you are as close to me as any brother. You have traveled the earth with me, gently reminding me, and guiding me, as unstinting as a father. You have watched me become as barren as the desert; then blooming as the flowers after the deluge. We have weathered many seasons together."

"Indeed, we have, brother." Tohami walked to one of the elders, lowering his head in whisper tones. As Tohami returned, I watched the elder attach the feather to one of the four direction poles rimming the wheel; the lapis stone crowning the sandstone in the middle of the wheel.

"Come, Angus, let us sit. The ceremony is about to begin."

Auburn flames danced and licked at the shadows of the chanting shaman inside the medicine wheel. Their slow staccato chants hypnotized me, wrestling memories from deep inside my mind, those that needed to be put to rest and released. I visualized them drowning in the sea of dirt and mud beneath the medicine wheel, deep into the core of the earth, burning and writhing in their demise, no longer able to haunt me, to scornfully taunt me.

An abrupt silence broke the spell. With my right eye slightly parted, I saw a girl's open-mouthed gasp, the scattering of people, a shaman's defeated outstretched arms, and finally, the glean of teeth, pearlescent, and of eye, vengefully bright. The alpha male of the wolves triumphantly stood over the oldest shaman, a mask of blood tingeing his muzzle. He called to the pack in monotone howls. I released my knife from its leather sheath on my left calf and barreled towards him, lunging into his chest. He lowered his head and bucked me in the gut, throwing me backwards toward the log seat I had been sharing with Tohami. The shrill yips of brave, young Dakota warriors deafened the chaotic screams swirling around me.

"Tohami! Tohami!" I bellowed hopelessly. "Zvezda! Nastooplieny! I bound across the medicine wheel, scattering pebbles and stones under my feet, watching bloody footprints trail behind me. Zvezda swooped in on the alpha male, her wings strained to their widest span and her talons poised to pluck the eyes from the beast. As she lunged, the male wolf yelped and jumped to nip at her tail feathers, but Zvezda circled the wheel and dove into the trees. With savage force, Zvezda whirled toward the male from his left side and plunged her sharp beak into his eye. His cry drove an eerie silence into the havoc.

Scanning the auburn faces of the Dakota, my ears drove my eyes to witness a scant pack of wolves at the edge of the medicine wheel, growling, digging and biting at something on the ground.

"Tohami! Tohami! I am coming to save you!"

The females and young males of the pack had Tohami pinned down, dusty balloons bellowing out from around his limp body. They pulled his arms and legs as a child pulls a rag doll, grinding their paws and muzzles into him. Above me, I felt a swift breeze quickly blowing up the back of my neck; I looked up—Zvezda. She screeched her warning to the wolves, exploding into the middle of the pack, scattering them in waves.

Falling to my knees, I reached for Tohami's face and turned it toward mine. His peaceful expression told me that I had been too late for my brother.

The Dakota have a funeral custom: they paint the faces of their dead red. It is considered the color of life, as the Dakota believe that the dead are reborn and enter a new life. In Russian culture, we often throw a copper coin in with the dead to assist them in redeeming themselves in a new world. I am not bitter; Tohami flies with me on the wings of eagles, and in the whisper of the wind I hear him say, "It is as it should be. Men accept this." The wolves had settled their score with me, and, such as the wolf accepts his nature in order to survive, I understood that in order to survive, I must also accept my true nature: lone wolfer.

About Jennifer Peckinpaugh

Jennifer Peckinpaugh is a Kentucky Native who lives with her husband and three children in Lexington, KY. A former acquisitions editor for the University Press of Kentucky, some of her successful titles include A Kentucky Christmas, Ginseng Dreams, Bees in America, *and* Appalachian Home Cooking.

The Monster and the Magician

by Johanna Lipford

"...that foul stynkyng lump of selfe ...between me and the Beloved..."
- The Cloud of Unknowing

Conflict slammed down his pencil, swept aside papers filled with equations and jumped up from his desk to hasten to Leroy Graves' office, to seek help from a man who might know.

"You busy, Roy?"

The director of research at Texas Scientific took his feet off his desk and straightened. "Never too, Cha'les. Come on in."

Charles slumped in a chair.

"Roy, I'd like to ask you a question..." He paused, working up the courage to reveal himself. "When you were in love with Marjorie, was there ever a time that...that you didn't...quite...feel you were in love with her?" Hope gazed at his friend.

Veiled grey eyes gazed back at him. Roy stroked his chin, "Mmmm—no. No, I can't really say there was. I finally left her... Well, I left her because I'd fallen out of love with her. I didn't realize it, at first. All I knew was that everything she did irritated me. She was slovenly, she was ignorant, her conversation bored me, and I began picking at her – trying to 'improve' her. And I didn't understand that I didn't love her any longer..."

"How did you understand that?" fear asked – he had been picking at Stella, he thought, loathing himself for a prig: among other things, they had quarreled over a university art exhibition he had insisted she see, and with an incomprehensible mulish stubbornness she refused even to set foot in it. And once, when he was reading her some favorite poetry she fidgeted, and fury acidly inquired if she were bored, and she replied "Yes – I had to study all that stuff at university". Snarlily he asked if that meant she need never read it again, and she retorted that if it didn't mean that, she didn't know why she had studied it, and they had quarreled.

"I saw a psychotherapist," Roy said. "He helped me see it." He paused. "If you're feeling... Well. If your feelings are confused, a talk with one couldn't hurt you any – and might be of use. Perhaps he could help you clarify them." He dryly chuckled. "It was strange – I knew she was in every way beneath me, I knew she was little more than a slut, I despised her, and yet I loved her insanely. It had to end, of course."

Charles left Roy's office with but one conviction: he would never see a psychologist. If one were to show him he did not love Stella he would not want to live. Because if he did not love her – if he did not love Stella! – then he was incapable of love. And – he groaned at the thought – if he did not love Stella he could not ever marry her; yet if they did not marry he would lose her... His thoughts leapt to Edith, he tried to recall his feelings for her and remembered only that she had come after Carol, who had dumped him, and that he had loved Edith for two days and had married her without loving her, though he had lied to himself that he did. Pity, and fear of being alone, had finally decided his marriage.

Was it the same thing after all? Stella and Edith? Loving Stella as he did he could not bear that he might someday marry her not loving her, and his stomach ached as if a knife were stuck in it.

Warm brown eyes full of love were looking into his.

A stomach aching with conflict had awakened him. He had taken off work and driven to the university to pick up Stella. They had just got in his car.

"O, I love you Carlo!" she burst out gripping his arm. "I love you so much!"

Agony had lived for months fearing he would never hear her say just those words. He bluely glared out at her from inside his prison, hating her for loving him when he could not feel he loved her.

"Don't! Please don't!"

"Don't what, darling?" She shrank back.

"Don't say you love me," hatred grated. "Don't call me 'darling'. Don't look at me, like..like that. I can't bear it!"

"But I love you, Carlo. Don't you understand? I want to tell you I love you, I want only to look at you, to touch you."

"Darling, I..I know, but – don't you understand? Don't you remember how you once felt? The way I feel now it's as if you're asking me for something I can't give, you make me feel— You make me feel.............. Just don't. Don't for awhile, until my feelings are...right, again."

"Impotent" had struck at him, to describe what he felt.

Anguish stared at him. She could not understand. She could not recall. Now that she so completely loved him, how could she recall an emptiness? Emptiness too was an emotional state, and therefore not real, had never existed, because it was not felt now. She saw only that she yearned to believe in his love, and that he perversely refused to let her. He did not love her, she thought dully. He would never love her again. Her eyes filled, she burst out—

"O, I hate you! O, how I hate you! O, God how could you? You made me love you, and now that I do, you don't love me! O Dio! Non ti voglio più vedere!" She pushed away from him. "Take me home at once!"

Misery dumbly looked at her. Frozen by the cold lump of himself congealed inside him, he could utter no tender word.

As he drove she sat pressed to the door, weeping. He longed to caress her, to tell her how passionately he loved her, but could not because seeing her tears over having lost him he despised her. They drove toward her apartment and her mother, his enemy. He dreaded their parting with poisoned hearts. They trembled on the verge of separating, and his body and mind and heart were one tortured nerve, thrilling with fear of loss. Abruptly he pulled the car to the side of the road.

"Stella, I can't take you home – not like this. I love you – God, I love you..and..yet.. what's happened? What has happened to us?"

She looked directly into his eyes and laughed without mirth. "I know what has happened. It is Mamma – working through me. She has destroyed us. It will never again be the same for us. Before she and I came to Texas she was the same with 'Tonio and me in Italy, and finally we decided never to see each other again. She has won."

Her mother was not at fault. He yearned to believe himself exhausted by the old woman's stubborn opposition to her daughter's seeing a divorced man, yearned to believe that Stella herself had destroyed his love the time she had abandoned him – yearned to believe any thing but what he feared: that he was incapable of permanent love. But he believed his heart mortally flawed, believed it peculiar to his self that once passion achieved its object, it vanished.

"No!" will declared. "I do not allow that! I will not lose you! I love you Stella!" Hearing his own words he felt their truth, ice in himself thawed and a torrent ran free and he passionately repeated, "I love you, I love you, I'll never leave you, I cannot lose you..." And they fell into each others' arms, mingling tears and kisses.

"Let's get married." His heart spoke unconsciously. It knew only that he had narrowly escaped losing her to that incomprehensible enemy in himself and that he must seize her now or risk losing her for good. "Let's go for the blood tests now. In three days we can marry – and in Texas we must marry within fifteen days."

She stared, amazed at the ease with which an insuperable barrier had been smashed through: he had vowed not to marry her for at least a year after they met, to ensure to himself – and to her – that he would know his heart. She grasped what his offer meant: that they must marry now, or might never, because he might never again trust himself enough to offer marriage, and she might never again trust him enough to accept.

"I..I..I don't know," bewilderment said, thinking of the Church. "I...I..yes. Yes! Let's get married!"

"It won't be a Church wedding." He hated to remind her. "But I promise you you'll have one, after the annulment."

"All right, Carlo." She saw, with something like awe, that he had become everything to her. To marry him she must sacrifice her mother, and now must even sacrifice the Church wedding she had always believed the only true marriage. And she would do this because she was pulled to it by that bond between them, that tough and fragile bond which was exactly as tough, and as fragile, as the two insuperable barriers that had just been smashed through.

Not allowing himself or her to think further, he drove to a medical center. The whole time they waited there he sat thinking, "Oh dear God, what have I done?"

Their blood let, he dropped her at her apartment and drove home, in terror of marrying her. He feared his self was incapable of matching the love she bore him. His self feared her and it hated her, for it sensed the danger in believing the loved one's love stronger than one's own. The self could rightly drown only in its own love for another. And now, again, he felt nothing – only dread he would marry her not loving her. He told himself that the physical love between them was enough, and contemptuously dismissed it. He wanted to feel love! He quit the apartment and walked rapidly to the campus, uncertain where he was bound.

On campus he headed toward the classroom where they had first met. It was past five o'clock. Charwomen and janitors listlessly pushed mops around plastic-tiled floors. The classroom was locked.

"Here!" He jammed a ten-dollar bill into a janitor's hand. "It's yours if you open that room and let me sit in it awhile."

The man stared into his hand. Without asking a question he drew out his keys.

Charles took the seat he had taken months before, when impulse had caused him to audit an Italian course. The janitor closed the door, and as Charles brooded in the gathering twilight the room thronged with ghosts. A woman with a severely beautiful face strode in, her blonde hair swinging on her shoulders, her green dress swinging about her hips...she stepped to the board and said "I am your Italian teacher, from Rome. My name is Miss Stella Draghetti...I shall write it for you..."

Amid the ghosts of himself, of the students, pain of loss sat. And he knew he would always be that, grasped that he had irreparably lost, a precious thing that could not ever be found again, and he burst into tears and sat weeping bitterly in the silent classroom as the ghosts, uncaring, unconscious, implacably pursued their motions around him. Desolation sat weeping for ghosts, for spent passion, for a love that was not, could not ever be, enough, because it was only love and not a desperate and all-consuming passion.

Back in his rooms, chained fast by his spiritual masturbation, he felt yet more bound to that foul stinking lump of his self. Stomach writhing with conflict he looked at faith, and at hope, and at love, and found no comfort for an empty heart. His mind was once more split on its old dilemma: "...I love her – but I don't feel I do; do I then love her? If I do not love her I cannot marry her – but if I do not marry her I shall lose her; but I cannot bear to lose her! But this must mean I love her...."

Pain-maddened as if a demon crouched at the base of his skull and pulled nerves from brain and spine he jumped up to pace frantically about. Pursued, panicked, once again he fled through the badlands of his past and this time in their arid reaches saw clearly a monster, one he had glimpsed before but turned away from in revulsion.

He remembered now how he had grown cold on Carol when he thought she loved him, and how, two days after he was sure Edith was his, he ceased to care for her; and he remembered that when Stella had first said she loved him he ceased to care for her too – until he found her love contingent on his defeating her mother. And now he knew she loved him with a whole heart, he had again ceased to care for her. All his love for her seemed to him fake, all his passion for her but unslaked desire for what he did not yet have, cold will that would have the thing it would have, and when it prevailed must then jettison its prize sucked of value. He looked long at the monster confronting him from his past, at its hundred heads and hundred coils, and felt faint with fright and loathing of this mouth and belly that would seize and gorge on a whole life, a whole world, and be yet unsated, was in fact insatiable, would seize and gorge and spew, gorge and spew again to gorge again and spew again, and again, and would yet gasp for more, for more, always for more...

Dismay gazed at this monster in himself, this monster of his self. It had to be fought, if not killed, subdued; and yet seeing this thing, this thing that could not be, his will failed, his heart failed, for he had not dreamed that any such thing could exist to be consciously fought in the modern world. For all such monsters had been made mythical, given a sanitary disguise: Freud had painted over their ferocity by explaining everything that man thought (except Freud himself, somehow not as other men) as mechanically determined because thoughts owed to self-serving mechanisms buried in the past and these mechanisms owed ultimately to the motions of atoms and the motions of atoms owed to yet smaller mechanisms inside the atoms, so that no place was left for conscious control.

And yet it was an age in which man also believed in his conscious rational control of nature, of his governments, of his science, of his machines, of his weapons. But behind all these things, yes, even behind Freud and the true things he had seen, lurked the untamed monster, a monster whose existence was denied, and when it was not denied, its consequences were. But Charles, trapped in his past, had surprised it, and he knew it was real, and as old and as evil as Hell.

How, he would come to wonder, could men hope to subdue the evil in the material world unless each man first subdued the evil of his own self? For only will could purposively manipulate matter, and the monster he saw, the untamed monster of the self leering at him from the labyrinth that gave it life, was the tainted source of all human will.

Looking at the obscene thing now, though he knew it must be dealt with, he at first capitulated, sure it was too strong to fight alone, sure he must summon a champion, and he thought at once of a psychologist. He would expose the monster to a psychologist, and pray to be exorcised, for he as yet believed the monster peculiar to him, and that a man could be exorcised of it by a talk with another man whose breast concealed a similar monster. Snatching up the telephone book he dialed a number picked at random, and made an appointment for the next day. Having seen the monster, he was so desperate now he would do anything to see it slain – even see a psychologist – anything, so long as he and Stella married within a fortnight. For were the wedding postponed it might never be held. He feared that were she to see his monster alive and voracious, she would no longer love him.

But the psychologist would somehow slay the monster and yet reassure him that he was in love with Stella. He would have to.

Wariness entered the psychiatrist's office clutching his coat close to his chest. Charles had taken a course or two in psychology, and had read casually in the field, but he still thought of a psychologist as a magician, a seer who knew all and saw all. Fear of the psychologist was indeed fear of what he would see in himself, and terrified of what he had glimpsed there, he vowed he would not let the psychologist talk him out of love.

The psychologist reminded him of Roy Graves: a man about forty, of middle height, slender, dark-complexioned, a sardonic curve to his mouth. Unlike Roy he looked weary, as a conscientious man who has seen too much of other men's folly and wickedness might look weary.

A few routine questions; then: "What's the trouble?"

Relief vomited it, emphasizing the conflict he was prey to, opening his coat and guiltily exposing a glimpse of the monster in his breast. Will concluded by announcing that come what may he would marry Stella in two weeks.

He sat back, expecting the psychologist to excitedly unsheathe Rorschach tests and thematic apperception tests, association tests and dream analyses, and hack at the monster with them. But the psychologist drew not a single weapon. Charles would afterward feel that the psychologist had seen too many men expose their monsters, that he had wearied of lopping the heads off monsters and seeing two heads grow where one had grown before, that he regarded men and their struggles with their monsters as faintly absurd. Charles would leave the sardonic psychologist with the unsettling impression that he had not been taken seriously, and on reflection would decide that not to take him seriously was the best anodyne the psychologist could administer – anodyne, because nothing short of death could cure him of being a human being.

"So," the psychologist now summed up. "You say you're going to marry this girl, in spite of everything – in spite of all these storm signals – because you love her?"

Defiance nodded, though blushing at the – perhaps unintended – irony. "I know I love her. It's just that I can't feel it. I don't know why. But I know that if I lose her – and I can lose her, I shall lose her if I keep… rasping her, as I am – it will be the greatest mistake I ever made in my life."

This was received by an utterly expressionless face.

"Don't – don't you think I love her?" weakness asked.

The psychologist shrugged. The psychologist lit a cigarette, and gazed at the ceiling. The psychologist studied his nails.

"You're an engineer, aren't you?" he irrelevantly asked. "Mathematician, that sort of thing?"

Charles nodded.

"And you like to be sure, don't you? – you like everything mathematically proven, exact, precise, nailed down. Isn't that so?"

Charles had never thought about it before. "No," reaction said. "I don't think so." For he hated the old cold precise unemotional self he'd imagined himself as, refused to recognize any connection with it. But he would later see that a desperate will to know exactly was one head of his personal monster.

The psychologist dismissingly waved a hand, and fell momentarily silent. Then he said something else irrelevant: "D'you know what a psychosis is?"

Charles understood it to be a state of mind in which one constructed a reality and lived according to it, even though it had little connection with the reality most people agreed on: "objective" reality.

The psychologist wearily nodded. "Exactly. Well, love – romantic love – is a psychosis. The lover constructs a picture of his beloved – a false reality – and lives according to that picture. Love ends when that picture – as it must, to an ordinarily sane man – finally reveals itself as not according with objective reality."

Superiority breathed an almost audible sigh: he had lost his fear of the psychologist. By that remark the wise and weary psychologist had revealed himself a fallible man. For who knew reality? Charles had spent six years in aerospace, a business whose foundation was supposed to be objective reality. But whenever that goblin was summoned to testify to itself by experiment, no two trained men could be found to agree on the reality underlying the bare observations made in never-unambiguous experiments by biased instruments that influenced as they viewed and reported with error. Roy was still seeking that experiment he could say had definitively proved something. Charles had seen physicists agree on reality by vote – as the Doctors of the Church had once agreed on the gospels. He had often seen reality constructed, but he had never seen it discovered. He had always preferred mathematical deductions to experimental inductions, because however unsupported by fact the deductions might be, they were anyway by God sure!

His distrust of the reality grasped through man's rational mind had only grown in the past months when he had been straining to discern the reality of his feelings for Stella, and had seen it slip like a globe of mercury under a thumb. He could only look upon as naive a man, or a profession, that believed objective reality to be other than a plastic human construction – however illuminating the man's non-rational insights into the psyche might be. The psychologist, relief saw, could not tell him whether he was in love.

And it struck him that cynical Roy had seen a psychologist, not to find out reality, but to construct it: he had come to be talked out of love. He had wanted to return to his wife and children, so he and his psychologist had constructed a reality in which he could: they had mutually decided on a definition of love such that, whatever Roy was, he was not in it.

But Charles had come to the psychologist to be told that he was in love with Stella, and fearing he was not, dreaded that an all-seeing psychologist would look at his self and inform him that whatever he might be, he was not in it. But the wise and the naive psychologist had now twice told him that no man could tell him. There was no experiment that could test his love for her, no mathematical proof to demonstrate it, no test that, after he answered sixty multiple-choice questions, would inform him that he was in love with her. There was no way to be sure. Not even feeling could tell him, because – as he had painfully discovered – feeling vanished when seriously doubted. So there was no way, except one: to believe that he was, on faith. And that illusion would create a reality in which he was in love with her, and because the monster willed also to love her he would believe that illusion.

And whatever neuroses, whatever complexes, whatever myriad mechanisms propelled his faith that he loved Stella, it existed, had existed, would exist, so long as he would believe it. He would not give it up, could not give it up, did not want to see a way he could give it up – would not look at the way were it shown him. The slave would love his dear bonds. He would love Stella. That was reality – and a free-floating and ungraspable reality it was, objectively.

"You know," the cynical psychologist observed, "love – romantic love – is perhaps the very worst basis for a marriage..."

At first insecurity would seize on this consolation prize: if (he would gingerly think) passionate love must be abandoned, why the domestic, affectionate love of marriage still remained, the love founded on knowledge springing from long association: the kind of love he had developed for Edith – still had. Still had. And that, passionless, had proved weak glue. He was quickly to realize that a marriage founded on that love was founded on the cant of social workers and psychologists, of those who loathed strong passions and unslaked wills because they were disorderly, chaotic, because they raised hell with conventions and rules, because they were explosive charges buried in a well-organized society – that material paradise on earth that the monsters buried in its believers, unslakably willed to realize.

The wise psychologist said one last thing: "Do you feel guilty, over having abandoned your wife and children?"

Charles thought. "No, I can't honestly say so – I've had too much else to feel."

The psychologist sardonically smiled. "Exactly. So don't be surprised if you begin to."

And Charles did. He was to become guilt, and have as his only weapon against his self the sure knowledge that he had done what was right, however evil it had been. Could he return, he would think, he would do exactly as he had done – only, he would feel everything more intensely yet, he would let no precious instant escape without experiencing it fully, for he would know that it all must end. And yet, he would understand too that ecstasy would not be ecstasy, if one knew it must end.

About Johanna Lipford

Born in San Francisco California, she grew up in San José. She worked as a mathematical analyst for seven years in the American aerospace industry: in Newport Beach California; in Boston Massachusetts; and in Austin Texas. At the age of thirty, having come to the conclusion that her life could not go on like that, she left aerospace. She spends her time between Austin Texas and Rome Italy. She has been writing for some time, but only recently has seen a number of her stories published.

Tropicana Blues

by Magda Knight

As soon as I enter the cordoned-off back room of the nightclub my nostrils are assailed by a heady aroma of flowers, old earth and blood.

It doesn't take a copcorder to tell me that the girl lying broken on the ground is a tea-rose, dark pink petals curled around her forehead in a close-knit cap and tiny ornamental thorns ridging the sides of her arms.

She is - or was - very pretty, and young. Too young to participate in whatever resulted in such a violent death. I make her out to be about twenty years old. About the same age as me, but then I'm police, so I've seen and done it all, and feel as ancient as the hills. She must have died a good few hours ago. Some of her petals lie on the ground, their edges curled, and her corpse is beginning to droop.

Lieutenant Solo is already bending over her, his handroots on the girl's feet, the first cop on the scene. It's part of what he does - extracting the dreams of the deceased to determine their cause of death. Part of his yew heritage, when travellers were warned not to sleep under the bows of a graveyard's most common tree too long, lest they never wake up. He's forensic. He's good with death and dreams.

"Hey, detective-lady."

The dim light of the nightclub suits Solo's yewish good looks. Tall, dark, handsome - he's got it all. And the dark humour to boot. Yep, him and me, we get on okay. He's too cynical for my tastes, though, and he tells me I'm too much of a greenshoot rookie for his. Thanks, Solo. Nice. Remind me to respect you too, sometime.

I nod him a hello. "Hey, Solo. What do you think?" Solo extracts his roots from the girl's feet, where her brains are.

"Not sure," he says. "She's got some holes, but I haven't figured out what made them yet."

He points out some tiny puncture wounds which curve round on the victim's cheeks in two tidy trails of incisions. My first thought is that a venus flytrap snapped this poor girl's face, but the marks are wrong, and the diameter's way too big for a flytrap, grotesque even - and anyway, we plants don't eat our own.

"Definitely not another hate killing," adds Solo and I breathe a huge sigh of relief. I trust Solo's talents. If he says it's so, then it's so. I can't help arguing, though. It's a birch trait. It's in my sap.

"You know what? Small mercy," I say. "If any more humans sneak over the water and murder one of ours, it'll escalate from floral riots to genocide. The humans'll dump a phoenix bomb on our asses and burn us into the ground."

"Quit the melodrama, Greensleeves," laughs Solo. He knows I hate it when he calls me that. It presses all kinds of buttons. "You don't really think fleshers would give up the sentient sativa parties? The florophilia? Humans love us!"

I shrug my shoulders. "Bub, you think everyone loves you. But time will tell. I say we're hanging by a thread."

Solo doesn't like this. Maybe it's because he's meant to be the cynical one. "Ah, Greensleeves. No more, no more. I'll tell you what I have found, though. The last thing this girl saw - the very last thing - was a gaping row of teeth."

Not much to go on, but already my brain is working overtime. I wriggle my toes to help me think, get the old green matter working.

"A row of teeth might explain those incisions down the girl's face. How big?"

"Big, Greensleeves. Big as your face."

"Human?"

"Don't be crazy, girl. What human has a mouth that big? They can't even swallow a field mushroom, let alone pop a young girl's head like it's a peeled grape."

He's got a point. I think sideways. Flytraps spring into my mind again - but no, forget it. An anti-hunch.

"Okay, forensic-man. Are we talking teeth as a euphemism here? What sort of imprint did you get when you poked around in her mind? Visual? Allegorical? Oral?"

Solo gets exasperated, now. "Sure, sister. Now why don't you go on and tell me the sound a gaping row of teeth makes? I'll tell you exactly what I saw. A cavernous maw, black inside, no tongue, seen from the victim's point of view. And teeth filling the periphery of my vision. Serrated. Double-rows. Not so much a death dream as a dream nightmare. And of course this was a visual imprint. Greenie, this was no dipsy-shit poetical representation of the victim's final fear. This is what she actually saw."

I can see Solo's serious about this one - and for all I rag on him, I know he's good at his job.

"You done good, Solo. With what you're telling me? There's a chance we might have an animalhead on the prowl. No tongue, more bite than a running chainsaw? I'm thinking it might be a fine afternoon for checking out the barrio, walking the streets, seeing if any of the sharkboys are going down."

Solo nods, once. "Greens, you do that. I'll go back upstairs, work the witnesses. Throw my weight around. I know this club, been here a few times. Never been kicked out yet. Maybe they'll trust a friendly face."

I know folks laugh about cops, and make themselves feel better and maybe safer by saying we're all about snacking in our cars and getting fat. But a cop is a cop, and when we make a decision? We make it fast.

And yet, as I make to leave, I'm held back, because something's gnawing at the back of my mind, not letting me go. The corpse on the floor is all wrapped up in her chalk outline like a quick and easy death takeaway, but even though it's a gruesome view, it's one I'm used to - so what, I wonder, is the thing that feels so wrong about all of this? I step forward to take a closer look at the girl, confidently stepping over the chalk outline because they're put there for citizens, not for cops like me.

She really does look beautiful. Far more beautiful than I do, it pains me to say. But then she's a flowergirl - they all look good. This one has the added benefit of looking almost human.

I bend down and gently touch her face, which feels limp and dry beneath my rooted fingers where it should be feeling plump and succulent to the touch. Our beauty is one of the reasons we're still alive as a species, I think. When the humans made us they spliced our genes with their own. They took gigantic risky leaps with our genes and theirs, with all the power and spoilt wilfulness of baby Roman Emperors. I can see why they did it, too. If you're a human, a pure, why have mere coitus when you can have sumptuous perfurmed sex with a flowergirl who never impregnates? Why have mere inebriation when you can smoke the dried and shredded skin of a sentient drug to immerse yourself in a mindblowing experience the like of which you've never even dreamed? Why spend a small fortune researching expensive medicines that only infrequently work when you can breed medicines that you can ethically say have been tested on humans - because they are part human?

I can feel Solo looking at me, keen to get on with things. But sometimes you can't rush a crime scene. You're not always aware of exactly what it is you're looking at, or looking for. You have to let your mind slip through the edges.

I need to slip through the edges.

So I half-close my eyes and look at the girl, wondering what my hunch is, this intuition that won't let go of me but equally won't rise up to introduce itself and give me a break.

Apart from the flowers and the stems and the roots, she looks human. What human would dare create a thing like this? Or kill it? That, I guess, is the crux of it. Why things got out of hand. Because we plantfolk, we propagated and mutated amongst ourselves. Flowers do it all the time. So do humans, for that matter. We picketed for rights, we plantfolk, once we'd learnt what they were. Sure, we were mostly harmless - but we gave new meaning to the term 'flower people', and eventually, unwillingly, the UN answered our call. We became an official species. A nation with many countries, isolated from the pures on Malta, England, Madagascar - any island that could be sealed off and mostly forgotten. Except for those exported callgirls and drugboys smuggled by pures to the mainland, we would never see another truly human face.

And everyone knows what happened to the other, animal-based experiments. And so I worry. As Solo would say, I worry a lot.

And then I get it. Yes... I see what it is I'm actually looking at, here on the chalked dirt floor. And of course it's blindingly obvious once I see it, and I feel like a fool for not noticing beforehand.

"Solo, check this out. The victim's blood is practically green, yet she looks almost pure human. Where's the human blood? What's with all the chlorophyll and none of the liquid brown?"

Solo gives me a sharp stare, like he's seeing me for the first time. "Good question. But appearances deceive, Greensleeves. We don't know for sure that she has a high purity percentage. What if she looks near-pure on the outside but on the inside she's an Immobile stuck in her greenhouse all day, waiting for someone to feed her?"

He knows how I feel about Immobiles. Got a soft spot for them. Always have, always will. And he's right, of course. But... I know my Immobiles, and this kid ain't one of them. I run a scan on her with the copcorder, because it's always good to have a second opinion.

"Rosie Fields. Waitress at Club Tropicana. Eighteen years. Minor paperwork for soliciting, but she's not in the big league - plant clients only, no humans. Tea-rose base, 30% human. Okay Solo, you'll admit there's nothing out of the ordinary there. Just your average citizen. So I ask again: why such an abundance of cholorophyll?"

"You're the detective, honeypot. I'm just forensics. Remember?"

It's a fair point. Solo's older than I am and has less to prove, which may be why he goes easy on me when I try to tell him how to do his job. Because I sure wouldn't stand for him trying to tell me how to do mine. So I let Solo go and talk to the potential witnesses. And for my part? Time to make like a tree and leave.

Ah, the barrio. The shit-stink hairpuke barrio. I decide to take the car. See, the animalheads, what few of them are left, live deep down there in the poorest part of the city. We plants have a lot of names for it. Animaltown. Dogsville. The Fleshpit. Dirty 30. All our names for the barrio are ugly, but all of them prettier than the place itself. I'm okay with animalheads, know a few of them even, but I've never felt comfortable around the bestial stink that follows them wherever they go. And the barrio is a mass of territorial spoors, piss and animal-flesh. I'd rather drive through that than walk any day of the week.

The heat of the day hits me with a full bodyblow as I walk down the front steps of the Tropicana and I start prickling all over from the nasty combination of wilting and sweat. I set off the car's mister to compensate - cool moisture caresses my leaves and I start to feel a whole lot better. I'm just about ready for some action now.

There's a street map on the front seat. I dunk it in the back. Cops always know their way around the poor parts of town - it's where they spend the majority of their time. I pass a street of greenhouses somewhere in the puzzle of narrow lanes lined with semi-decrepit buildings that collar the edge of Animaltown. The greenhouses are filled with Ingrowns, also known as Immobiles, silent and unmoving. It always does me good to see Ingrowns looked after - these ones, well, their greenhouses may not have all the mod cons, but from the overhead sprinklers and the unsmashed windows it looks to me like they do okay. Ingrowns are a cop's favourite citizen because they're fine and upstanding by their very nature. They're called Ingrowns - or Immobiles - because they're far more plant than human - hell, they have less than 5% human in them, not nearly enough to commit a crime. Some people see Ingrowns as throwbacks and look down on them. Not me. Ingrowns have whispering leaves, and croon with pleasure when they're fed by the water brigade, and yowl with pain when vandals set about their unprotected roots with knives. Ingrowns are innocent. I like Ingrowns. Always have, always will.

The closer I get to Animaltown, the more the air around my car is tinged with stratospheric layers of guilt, suspicion and fear.

Every time I look at a face in a doorway it darts away. No-one wants the long bough of the law to come down righteously upon them. A few raggedy catkids pull out their keys at a traffic light, like they want to scratch my paintwork but their claws aren't sharp enough for the job - I eyeball them and they bound away. The copcar's attracting too much of the wrong type of attention. I park on a relatively safe side street and activate the aphid security system, reasoning that a badged tree walking the streets is a lot more friendly than a badge riding separate from the have-nots in a marked car. Hey, I'm all about the community spirit - even if it does mean I have to stop myself from holding my nose as I navigate these foul-smelling, feral and clotted streets.

I head gingerly through the backstreets of Animaltown, picking my way through pelts drying on balconies, groups of excitable youngsters with prehensile tails and moist-eyed beggars standing on four legs instead of two. Signs in shop windows saying 'Carnivores only - no Osmosarians allowed'. I wish Solo was here, or one of the streetcops. A little plant company would make me feel easier. But some things you have to do alone. I know what I'm looking for, anyway: A guy called Mouth Mako who owns a slightly sleazy but colourful fish restaurant called Finn McCool's. He's my friend, of sorts. He's also my first lead.

Finn McCool's. Lying just ahead of me. A ramshackle little place, but a bit of lick and spit has gone into its upkeep, you can tell. Peering through its net curtains reveals to me a fairly healthy shoal of customers. A romantic couple placed by the window (a silvery-backed part-mackerel and a young lady with more than a trace of seahorse) look up to see me gawking at them, spot the police department badge atop my foliage and hurriedly look back down into the cheap wriggling '2-for-1' contents of their bowls.

It takes my eyes a moment to adjust to the gloom as I go inside. It's still hot although the day's beginning to fade - but at least it's nicely air-conditioned in here. I hadn't been expecting its owner to fix the air conditioner when I'd moaned about the heat on my last visit. He must have listened to me.

I scout around, and finally see Mouth Mako, the restaurant's owner, sitting flanked by waiters at a table at the back of the restaurant, near the bar. He's old and infirm but he masticates joyfully at his meal, which consists of a live young atlantic sea pup that his waiters try to hold down for him on the cheap checked tablecloth that is now spattered with more than one kind of red. The seal pup squeals and thrashes as old Mako delves noisily into its innards. As a plant, it makes me feel all kinds of ill to see meat downed like that, and I have to remind myself I'm a cop, each culture to its own and all that, and at least it's organic - let's face it, you can't get food much fresher.

Mako spots me, and I momentarily shiver as he looks up - his eyes look so cold and dead when you haven't seen him for awhile, the eyes of a killer. But then I did have the cheek to interrupt him during feeding time, I suppose.

"Greensleeves! Oh, the pleasure!" As one of the waiters dabs his pinkly frothing mouth with a napkin he pushes them off and totters over to greet me, craning to peck me on the cheek.

"Oh, bend a little lower miss Greensleeves," he groans. "The arthritis."

One of his customers, spotting him as the patron of the place, beckons Mouth and asks for shrimp.

"Are you kidding?" moans the Mouth. "Oh, how you hurt me! This may be a fish restaurant - but it is a kosher restaurant!" The customer, a grouchy pinkmeat salmonhead, grumbles and walks away.

Mako the Mouth's eyes look weepy and geriatric now, and filled with yellow gunk. A little worse than when I last saw him. I should try to score him some medicine. And I don't mind him calling me Greensleeves - he's a nice old shark.

"Hey, Mako. How's it hanging?"

"Very good, very good..." he motions at the dive's customers busily eating away.

Mako ushers me over to a table in a private corner, then calls for a waiter to bring me a basin of cool mineralised water. Unlike many of his Animaltown neighbours, Mako's no segregationist. He welcomes plant customers as much as any other kind. Because he had the narrowest of escapes in the near-genocide of the animal/human experiments, Mouth Mako has no desire to make an enemy of anyone. He may be based on the ultimate predator, but in today's society, he's an endangered species. Oh, yes. Mouth Mako: altruist, informer, restauranteur... a cop's wet dream, and a sweet old guy to boot. I thank him, place my feet in the basin and begin to drink.

"So what is it you want?" asks Mako gently. He's helped me a few times. I've helped him a few times. Every cop on the beat has a friend like Mako.

Before I answer, I study his teeth. Mako has the jaw of a shark, most definitely, and his double-rowed teeth have a huge span. But they look pretty blunt to me, and I doubt they could be the maw seen in Lieutenant Solo's vision, the one that killed Rosie Fields with those tiny incisions and did something strange to the blood that used to course through her veins.

"There's been a murder," I say. "A flower girl down at the Club Tropicana. Bite marks. Know of anything going down? You know me, Mako - you know I don't want bad juice betweeen our species. If you know anything, I'll get the most lenient sentence on the perpetrator I can - and I'll hush it up. No-one outside Animaltown will ever hear of it. That's my promise."

Mako says nothing. The way he looks at me? It's wrong.

Bzzt. Bzzzzt. My copcorder goes off. I place it on the table between us.

"Calling all cops - shark-based perp on the run in Animaltown between East Street and Thurley Lane. Armed and dangerous and wanted for murder. Calling all cars - repeat - calling all cars."

I'm not expecting what happens next. There's an empty click in the air. I feel rather than see my instincts kick in, and Mako's jaws snap shut where my hand and copcorder used to be. If I hadn't shoved myself to one side, he would have splintered both. Mako, no! He's coming after me again, sharkhead down like a battering ram with a steel edge. I bound away into a corner - too far away from the exit, a bad decision, but I've got a clear view of the whole room.

A waiter pulls out a knife and throws it skillfully at my feet. Aiming for my brain. I sidestep and shoot his damn hand off, but then Mako chases me again, head down and mouth wide open. It's risky but I'm desperate so I hold out my right arm and splay out my finger-roots as far as they will go, throwing them over his jaw like a net. Mako struggles to pull free but my tree-strength wins out - for the moment. If he was a younger shark I wouldn't have stood a chance.

With my other hand I fire a warning shot into the ceiling. The customers scoot under their tables. The waiters are slower to comply.

"Everybody - down on the ground!" I bark.

The waiters aren't throwing knives, but they're not getting on the ground, either.

"Hey, waiters!" I yell. "I'm not going to hurt Mako, I promise." He struggles at this, but I manage to hold him fast.

"Waiters, get outside. Stand out the front like you're having a cigarette break - where I can see you. No running off for help. You do that, something bad will happen."

I can't bring myself to say I'll hurt Mako, but one hand tightens on his face, and one hand tightens on my gun, and I think they know what I'm trying to say. They finally leave the room. Now that the room is cleared I can concentrate on Mako properly. I shift my grip on his face a fraction of an inch.

"Will you behave if I let you go?" It hurts me, but I point the gun at Mako's face as I say it.

He nods, and his eyes look like the eyes of an old man, sad and rheumy. I tentatively let go. He inches back to show compliance, then - surprisingly and upsettingly - bursts into tears.

I don't know what to do. I hear the distant wail of police sirens, but it's hard for cars to navigate Animaltown's streets because, being the scrag-end of town and filled with animals, they're both narrow and clogged up with crap.

I hesitate then guide the weeping Mako into a chair. Clasping his head in his hands, shoulders heaving, he is unable to look at me.

"I'm so sorry," he blurts. "So very sorry."

He holds out his hands. "I understand you are a good officer, Miss Greensleeves. Please, handcuff me now."

I know he's just tried to snap my arm off, but my heart can't help but go out to the poor old guy.

"What's happening, Mako? Please. Tell me."

"It is my son," he quavers. "I find a gun in my son's closet. Every day, it is there, so I say nothing. Today it is not there. This murderer - it is my son!"

There's a bang outside. People shouting. I look up to see the waiters scattering in the path of an approaching figure, and I register incredible power and speed as he shatters the restaurant window and bounds through. It is Mako's son. Blue Steel. 300kg of prime manshark, glistening scales pulled tight over hard, fast meat. He assesses the situation and shoots, but it goes wide and hits his father. Blood spurts out of Mako's shoulder. His eyes open wide.

Blue Steel freezes, shakes his head, makes to shoot again, but he's too slow. Firecracker pops sound all around me, again and again, and Blue Steel falls to the ground like a ship's heavy anchor. Dead weight.

My first thought is to make sure Mako's okay but he totters off and collapses on the body of his son, wheezing and wailing out a shark song of mourning, an ocean keening. And they say sharks don't feel. Twenty cops stand around Blue Steel's body, now. They'll never know who shot him. Not until they sit down and count the bullets.

Someone steps through the door and comes towards me briskly. It's Lieutenant Solo. His eyes brighten in recognition when he sees it's me.

"Solo?" It's the only question I can think to ask.

"I shouldn't be here. I know. Forensics don't do firefights. But I was in the area, and a streetcop needed a ride."

He looks swiftly over at Mako. I know he is friends with Mako, too. Is there any cop who isn't?

"Mako, sir, I'm sorry. Your son was wanted for the murder of his girlfriend, Opal Shoals. Did you know her?"

Mako wails harder. Solo looks morosely at me - no cop likes this part of the job - but continues.

"It seems it was a crime of passion, Mako. Don't worry. An ambulance is on its way. We'll do everything we can." They're kind words, but Mako can't hear them above his keening, and anyway, everyone in the room knows that Blue Steel is dead.

Time to be a cop. I kneel down next to the grieving shark. "Anything you want, I'll be there," I say softly. Even it means skipping work to go to Blue Steel's funeral, I add quietly to myself, feeling it's not yet the right time to say it out loud. Then I get up to go and have a private talk with Solo, ignoring the other cops as they file into the fish restaurant to start the procedure, the ritual of note-taking and photo-matching and witness-questioning.

"Hey, forensic-man," I say. "Mouth Mako doesn't know anything, and his son didn't murder Rosie Fields, whoever else he may have murdered. His teeth are sharper than his father's, but still not sharp enough to produce the incisions on Rosie's neck."

"Well, you tried. Anything else to go on?"

"Nopeski. Sorry, Solo. Dead end."

"Come on, Greensleeves. Any hunches up those green sleeves of yours? You detectives, you've always got something cooking on the back of the stove. What about the chlorophyll content in that blood?"

His tone is teasing - I mean, me and Solo have this thing going on - but I wonder why he's pushing so hard. But then I remember.

"It sounds crazy-mad, I know," I say. "But I was thinking about venus flytraps. I know they don't move much, and they've got a small mouthspan - and, well, hell, they're just insect-munchers. But unless those incisions were made by some kind of customised weapon then a flytrap is the only plant I can think of that even comes close to creating those marks we saw."

Solo draws out a long low whistle. "Greensleeves? With you, nothing is impossible. This forensics expert, he says 'yes'. You going to check up on it? Maybe see if there's a link with the Tropicana?"

"Well, sure," I say. But I have to admit I'm a little puzzled. Because Solo has never been this obviously supportive of my cop skills before. I'm not entirely sure I'm comfortable with it.

He gently catches hold of my arm, and I feel his rough, darkly-knotted yew bark press gently then more firmly against the relative smoothness of my birch.

"Greensleeves," he says. Then looks as if he's about to say something else, but changes his mind.

"Be lucky, okay?" Then he speeds off somewhere into the night, to do whatever wild and dark things I suspect it is he does in his free time. And I find myself surrounded by bullet holes in the walls, and one young dead shark, and one old shark that might as well be dead. And even though I should be taking charge I'm just standing in a sea of busy activity and officiousness and family tragedy and crackling copcorders relaying orders, and thinking about Solo's touch and Solo's words and wondering what the hell just happened.

It's dark by the time I get back to HQ. Photosynsthesis time. The streets will be quieter now, as all good citizens sleep, but there's no rest for the wicked - or for the boys and girls in green who police them with all their might. I head for one of the department's photosynthesis chambers, which gets a night's worth of photosynthesis done in ten minutes. Although not as effective as a good night's sleep, it keeps you on your feet through the small hours and means we can do shift-work. I don't like these chambers much. You always come out feeling a little woozy, a little slow.

While I'm photosynthesising, my copcorder runs me up a list on all the venus flytraps in the city. It's a short list. Most of the flytraps are Immobiles, kept in the Floralogical Institute at the Imperial Gardens. With no sexy qualities and no hallucinogenic or medicinal properties coursing through their stems, venus flytraps were not really used as experiments by humans. Some were used for war, I think, but it never worked out. I mean, a flytrap just sits around and catches bugs. What good is that?

There are a couple of Mobiles on the list, but not many. It should be pretty easy to visit them tonight and gather enough leads to work with in the morning. There's a Flora Perrez in Scoot Street (my heart jumps when I see the name. Scoot Street! Place of my birth! I'm going home!) and there's a Manuel Verdo down on Memory Lane, in the outskirts of the city. I'll just have to hotroot it to each one in turn and see what stones I can turn up.

The evening is calm and breezy. There's a low pollen count tonight, crackles the news through the copcorder. Whoop! A low pollen count is sweet, sweet news to the cops - flowers are peaceful folk when their sap isn't rising. A flower on heat and not getting any can be a dangerous thing, for sure.

It's a nice journey. All too soon, I'm there. The Florological Institute was a museum of some kind before this island became a country of flowers. It rises up in the moonlight, crumbling white wedding-cake stone surrounded by tended parkland, ornamental lakes and tall, dark Immobile cedars and oaks eradicating my view of the straight lines of the city. The Institute's walls are broken and fuzzy with the healthy, clambering bodies of Immobile creepers, making the place look like some old temple chanced upon in deep jungle. Lilies lie in profusion on the pond by the main entrance. One lazily waves a tendril in greeting as I enter.

You can feel the love in this place. Every available spot is covered in green - plant pots, stacked shelves, channels cut into the floors - everything proliferating with Immobiles, plants with only just enough human in them to be a step up from our venerable ancestors, all keening with pleasure as they are fed by the Bindweed and Dog Mercury technicians who wander the halls in their white coats, adjusting mineral levels and taking notes. The technicians all look a little sleepy - they'd probably rather be tucked up and photosynthesising.

I step in front of a very intelligent-looking young Dog Mercury, placing a root on his vinyl notepad to interrupt his work.

"I'm here on police business," I say. "I need to talk to someone about venus flytraps. Who's the best person for the job?"

The technician rubs his eyes but seems friendly enough. "Doctor Santiago. Miss, he's the best person for any job."

He passes his notepad onto a colleague then takes me through a monkey-puzzle of corridors until we come to a halt outside Doctor Santiago's office. The Dog Mercury hovers, uncertain as to whether he should stay or leave.

"It's fine," I say. "I'll take it from here."

It's very dark inside Doctor Santiago's office, with a smell of learning in the air. When my eyes adjust to the gloom I see him standing motionless in a corner of the room on a soil bed, photosynthesising, but despite his lack of movement there's nothing Immobile about the man. Pale fluid bark, handsome greying features - I'd say the good Doctor is about 60% human. Only the sprouting twigs and spring shoots give him away. It pleases me somehow that a man so human could care so much for his Immobile cousins. Gives me hope for us all.

The Doctor's eyes snap open when I cough. He steps off his earthy bed immediately.

"Yes, detective. Can I help you?"

Oh, very good. He's not only spotted the insignia of my badge, he knows what it means. Quick thinker. Without going into too much detail, I explain I'm on a case, and ask if he can help me understand how venus flytraps work.

Doctor Santiago doesn't ask any questions. He's all about sharing his knowledge, this man. A real find. I'm ushered over to a bank of CCTV screens and he points out one that shows the venus flytraps in the Institute, all cohabiting in the one room. They're all Immobile. They're static for the most part, but every now and then one of them snaps, trapping one of the flies buzzing round the room like a small dark blizzard on the cctv.

"Are venus flytraps carnivores?" I ask.

"They're plants," says Doctor Santiago, "and feed like normal plants. But they grow in poor soil, and the protein from the insects they catch supplements their diet. They've been mythologised and built up, but they're hardly the monsters that some make them out to be."

Another trap springs shut on the screen.

"Less than a second," says Doctor Santiago softly.

I decide to risk it. "Do you think there's any way a venus fly trap could be a murderer, or be used as a murder weapon?"

The Doctor looks at me with surprise. "Heavens, no! Murder is an ethical word. Could a flytrap kill an insect? Yes. Could it murder a sentient plant? Impossible. You can see for yourself that all our Immobiles are tiny. They just don't get very big! And flytraps make highly imperfect killing machines. If they spring shut on an insect that is too large for their trap, air gets in and moulds form around the trap's interior until it drops off and dies! This is hardly a way to murder anything larger than a very small pebble, detective!"

The Doctor is excitable. I don't think he likes the idea of plants murdering anything. I try a different approach.

"A girl was murdered today. She had two tiny trails of incisors around her face." I show him a photo on the copcorder. "What could it be?"

Doctor Santiago stares thoughtfully at the photo. "I see why you thought maybe a flytrap could have done it. But they do not have double rows of serrations, only the one around the lip of the trap. This is true of all cases. And no flytrap, as I said, would be big enough. Also - they are not bloodthirsty killers. The insects merely supplement their diet. What else could it be, do you think?"

"I thought something shark-based might have been the killer," I say truthfully. "But sharks aren't necessarily killers, either. And their teeth are too big to create such tiny incisions. Sorry, Doctor. I have to get going. Anything else you can tell me about flytraps before I take my leave?"

"Not really, detective. They are exotic. They are pretty. They entice insects in with their pretty colours. They are rarely fast enough to catch the insects they need. I don't like this idea of plant murder, I must admit. It makes me feel uneasy."

"Me too," I sigh. "Me too. Thank you. I'm sorry to have interrupted your photosynthesis. I'll be on my way now. And thank you for showing me the flytraps... you're right, Doc, they're very beautiful!"

"It amazes me, what a rich world we live in sometimes," says the Doctor, breaking into the first smile I've seen since waking him. "I like to share it, and maintain it if I can. Goodbye, detective. And may I say you're one of the finest silver birches it's been my pleasure to meet?"

A near-human! Complimenting 'me', a mere birch! I blush to the roots of my core.

"No problem, Doctor. Take care."

Heading on back to the car, I surreptitiously view my reflection in a window. A long crown of silvery leaves grows down my head and back and shoulders. Trim human physique, my favourite feature. No need for clothes - my bark comes over and across my legs and arms and torso and ends in a ruff round my neck. Green for now, my greensleeves are, but they'll be silver one day. Hell. Before puberty, I used to look a lot more human than this. I cast my eyes away, and hurry along. Because my next stop will be Flora Perrez, the mobile flytrap on my list. I feel a quickening of excitement in spite of my night-time sleepiness. I'm going home! The copcorder gives me a quick rundown as I speed through the city streets: Flora Perrez, 57, venus flytrap - 26% human. Previous profession: charlady. No current employment. Current residence: 18 Scoot Street.

Oh, how I love Scoot Street. Its thickwalled buildings and sunny lawns are etched into my stem cells and burnt into their green, green nuclei, for Scoot Street is the poor yet unpretentious place where I grew up, where most people want to leave, and most people stay.

As I get closer and closer to the gardens I used to call my home - before I became a cop - my car almost imperceptibly slows down. It'll be good to see my dad again, but it's always hard to go back to your roots.

And there he is, swaying on my front lawn as he has done all my life. I love him to bits, my dad. A fine old silver birch, his delicate leaves rustling in the breeze. Immobile, but fatherly and wise nevertheless, I'm sure of it. I'm angered to see a branded plastic bag from some chainstore tangled in his feet - doesn't the water brigade pass by these days to take care of things? I remove it and jump up to give him a big hug, and I kiss the knotty lumps I like to call his face for good measure. Hello, dad!

His woodpipes make an oo-oo sound, one I've learned to associate with pleasure. Poor dad. I know you couldn't do much when I lost my friends at school, changing with puberty from a popular near-human to an average treegirl with leaves in her hair and a rough bark body. Poor me, too - it's hard for a sapling to realise her youthful dreams of entangling lovers' bodies (moans, whispers, sighs and promises and pounded caresses on satin sheets) will not, it transpires, ever amount to anything more than a kiss, the entwining of boughs and some mutually-desired pollination. Far more practical, perhaps. But - since I've not yet experienced pleasure with another of any kind - an option that sounds far, far less romantic.

No, dad, I know you couldn't help me through all of that, stuck as you were in our lawn and dependent on us feeding you and keeping you entertained - but you did show me what a fine thing it can be to be a tree. For that I'm grateful.

A small sigh escapes my lips, issuing from woodpipes spliced with fleshy vocal chords. Yep. In every sense a complicated sound.

Another family hug, and then I get moving. Today's case has been guiding my every step, and Flora Perrez is just down the street.

Her house surprises me, I have to admit - it's ridiculously easy to locate since the front door is wide open, the lights are on, and the sound of smoky but lively jazz comes from within. It's vivacity contrasts heavily with the dark silence of the rest of the street, and I'm reminded of the nocturnally active flytraps on the Institute's night-time cctv, hunting for flies while all other good citizens bury their poor weary rootheads deep beneath the earth, lost deeply in their dark, soil-enriched dreams.

"Detective Birchfield here," I call. "Anybody home?"

"What is? Who is?" calls a voice from inside the house. I hear more than a trace of foreign accent in those rich tones.

"Hi, Mrs Perrez? I'm Sam Birchfield's daughter from down the street..."

As soon as she bounds into view I can tell she's an exotic specimen. In her late fifties, Mrs Perrez is draped in a bright dynamically-patterned evening dress with iridescent beetle-shells threaded into her hair, but she comports her fat and aging body with the carriage of an ex-dancer, one hand snapping with alacrity at a moth while she wipes the other hand on her dress.

"You said you was detective?" Mrs Perrez scrunches up her face doubtfully.

"But I'm not here in any official capacity," I hasten to reply. "I came to see my dad, and saw your light on, and..."

"Yes, come in!" beams Mrs Perrez. These exotics, they're so much more familial than temperate plants. I have a feeling Mrs Perrez might be a sucker for sharing gossip. Maybe I could use that.

"Your father, Sam, he is nice tree, lovely man. You need see him more! I live here two years now, I never see you before..." She pulls me into her drawing-room, smelling faintly of perfume and sweat - maybe she was dancing to the music now bouncing off the walls? Very expressive, these exotics.

"From now on you visit me when you visit your father, okay?" suggests Mrs Perrez. "We old ones get so bored, so tired..."

"I can't imagine you being tired in a million years, Mrs Perrez," I say, glad to be ushered into the near-inescapable depths of a fat armchair. The night has always felt like beddy-bye-time to me, and the police photosynthesis chambers at HQ can only go so far to mitigate that. Just looking at indefatigable Mrs Perrez makes me feel exhausted. "Mrs Perrez, you are not tired. You're living the nocturnal jazz dream while the whole world lies in its soilbed!"

"We flytraps no need sleep, you lovely girl!" says Mrs Perrez fondly, swaying her hips in time with the music. I think she's taken me to her petally bosom in all but the most literal sense. "We get extra power from the meat; it makes us muy fuerte, extra strong... My hands are dainty as a girl's, but they are fast, look!"

Mrs Perrez snaps her pretty, tiny claws like green, click-clacking castanets. I notice they wouldn't even fit round poor Rosie Fields' wrist, let alone her broken head. These hands as murder weapons? Impossible.

Mrs Perrez - or Tia Flora as she now insists I call her - snaps at another moth while she brings me a basin of delicious mineralised water. Poor people can be very houseproud.

"I am fat because I am old, but also because I am so greedy!" she laughs. "I catch many insects, especially in summer. My last job is cleaning for rich family. They like me cleaning when they sleep, because then in morning they have beautiful house, yes? It makes sense. But then their youngest daughter, not so pretty, she is trying to pollinate, and she is finding it hard. None of the boys want her, you know? The lady of the house, she say I eat too much, I eat the insects that bring her daughter the pollen from her many suitors. Oh, the mother lie to herself, her daughter has no suitors! She is too ugly! Her mamma fire me for nothing!" Mrs Perrez sighs noisily.

"So, my dear, I eat a few flies, even so. I cannot help myself. They are so rich. What do they care about a few flies? But no, the lady she no likes this, and so I lose my job. But never mind. My daughter keep me, and I find another job anyway!"

"It sounds like you have a very good daughter, Mrs Perrez. Does she do night-work like cleaning too?"

Mrs Perrez - Flora - Aunty makes a little moue of purse-lipped disgust and I could almost believe she is angry, though she snorts with amusement.

"Guapo Dio! You think my daughter needs to clean? My beautiful daughter is 92% human!"

I gasp. That much rich red human blood in her veins and the daughter still resides in Plant City and visits her charlady mother every night? She could have caught the first plane out. She could be living the high life as a human, wearing a string of rich men round her neck and sipping vinegared pearls. I'm beyond jealous.

Seeing the shocked expression on my face that she was no doubt expecting, Mrs Perrez hauls out a photo album and drops it on my lap. She figures it right: I'm a happily captive audience. So I browse through the photos, looking for clues: looking for anything. There is Juliette Perrez as a peaches-and-cream baby. There is Juliette clutching her first toy. There is Juliette as a sweet little golden-haired girl playing on a swing at her birthday party, swinging the swing with chubby little five-fingered, fingernailed hands while her little flower-friends look up in admiration, like daisies turning their heads to the life-giving sun. There is Juliette dressed up for the school fertility ball, her smooth human skin a perfect green. Green? I raise an eyebrow at her mother.

"Doesn't my daughter look beautiful as a sapling? I mean, teenager?" she demands. I comply. "She is green now, of course, beautiful green skin, extraordinary green hair. But not leaves, you understand? Hair." Mrs Perrez's eyes mist over as she hugs the photo to herself. "Oh yes. Green eyes. Green hair. A special girl, my Juliette. Such a good daughter. And 92% human! Who would have believed it?"

"I do," I say. "Your daughter is most truly beautiful. She clearly doesn't need to work as a cleaner, so what does she do? Does she make use of her near-purity in some way?"

Mrs Perrez leans back in her chair. A pinpoint spotlight of burning pride flares in her eyes. "Can it be you do not know? She has the most perfectly-formed vocal chords in this country. If you did not work so hard, I think you would have seen her perform by now. My Juliette is so talented... I tell you now, she is the famous La Verda."

"La Verda?" I ask. It appears to be a stupid question.

"The singer, child, you know? The famous singer. La Verda. Madre Dio, I can't believe you do not know."

"Is she on the television?" I ask timidly.

Mrs Perrez makes a *pffft*. "Does television have timbre, child? No! My Juliette performs live. She is La Verda, the famous singing star."

"So where does she perform?"

Mrs Perrez looks at me as if I were mad. "Are you crazy? Can it be you really have no idea? At the Club Tropicana."

* * *

I don't even bother going to see Manuel Verde, the third flytrap on my list. It would be pointless - the wheels are turning full circle, now.

I head back to the Club Tropicana. I'm driving as fast as I can, beyond the speed limit even, but no speed I hit seems fast enough. It is only when I see the club's neon lights smeared through the rain on my windscreen that all the anticipation leaves my body and I feel slow, slower than a riverbed shunted by gravity and water and time. But I'm a cop, and even if we have moods and passions, we don't let them affect our work. Not the good cops, anyway, so I get out of my car and climb the steps to the club's front door. It's locked, but one of my handroots is carved every day by official police manicurists into the shape of a skeleton key so I get into the club without any problems. An alarm sounds, so I alert HQ with the copcorder and they turn off the alarm. Being a cop makes things so easy.

I don't need to switch any lights on inside the Tropicana because it's already illuminated, clusters of little glowbugs revealing the sumptuous red carpet. The air of the club is laced with the scent of perfumed flowermolls and rich old tobaccopappas. This club sure is a top joint and no mistake. I prowl over to the side of the foyer to what I assum to be the coatroom - like the ticket office by the front door, there's no-one there. A pool of light leads down the stairs, and looking up them, all the lights on the first floor are switched off. Whoever's here is downstairs, then. I head down and find myself in a narrow corridor. Some of the doors have stars on them, and I may be out of touch when it comes to the niceties of contemporary public entertainment, at least as far as Mrs. Perrez is concerned, but even I know what a star on a door means when I see one.

I don't want to make my presence felt, because to be honest I'm too frightened - isn't everyone frightened when they find themselves in an unknown place, all alone? But I'm used to this feeling, so I call out to let whoever else is here know that I'm here, too, because the cops of Plant City pride themselves on making the presence of justice felt with words and mutual respect, not guns.

Oh yes. I'm unarmed. I've not had time to reload, and that nasty scene in Mako's fish restaurant used my last bullet.

One door is slightly open and I push it open all the way and walk in. A very beautiful woman is seated inside at a dressing table. Not quite as young as me, but a whole lot prettier. She looks like an old film star as she dabs her nose with some expensive-looking kind of cream and crosses her legs under a floor-length black silk dress. Just imagine the number of silkworms that died to make that. She must be used to being stared at, because she sees me come in and doesn't say anything, just carries on taking off her make-up as if she has all the time in the world.

I see something else on her dressing table but it makes my heart lurch; I don't want to think about that right now. It's a photo.

"Hello Juliette," I say.

Her mother was right - Juliette Perrez is absolutely stunning, and completely human. The wetness of her eyes, the soft stranded sheen of her tresses, the legs she just crossed with the five painted toenails on each foot - coupled with these, the green skin and hair just seem designed to make a human wish they could drop that irksome 5% humanity and thus look as wonderful as her.

"Mm?" says Juliette. The sound is as non-committal as it is melodious.

It's tricky. I know she murdered Rosie Fields. I just don't know how, or why.

I say the first thing that comes into my head.

"You're not on the list."

"Mm?" says Juliette. "I'm on everyone's list. I'm La Verda. The question is, who are you?"

I snap into cop-mode. "Detective Skinner Birchfield, ma'am. Of the New England Police. Can you explain to me why your mother is a venus flytrap - why you yourself are a venus flytrap - and yet you're not on the comprehensive list of venus flytraps held on the city files?"

"But I'm not a venus flytrap," says Juliette Perrez. "I'm human. What are you doing here?" She should sound scared or at least curious. Instead, she sounds bored.

"You're not human!" I shout. I know why I'm shouting. It's that photo on her dressing table. It presses all kinds of buttons. "You're a plant! You're 8% plant! That makes you a plant in plant terms, in human terms - in anyone's terms but your own."

"So what?" says Juliette. I have to concede it's a damn good point. I don't seem to be getting anywhere. Fortunately for me - or perhaps unfortunately, considering how things pan out - she stands up, and from her wonderfully expressive face she appears to be getting somewhat annoyed herself.

"Check the other list," she continues angrily. "I am human - I am so!"

She nearly has me there, until I remember.

"There isn't any other list, Juliette! Humans don't live here. There's no point having records on a species which doesn't exist in this country."

Juliette Perrez comes closer. "Well, maybe there is, in fact, another list," she hisses softly. "Have you thought about that, detective? A list for people who aren't plants, who aren't humans, who don't fit in any way at all, who are just... ?"

She's very close to me now, and I take a step back.

"What do you mean?"

She doesn't say anything now, which is odd because her mouth is opening. In fascination I see Juliette Perez open her mouth wider than any human could until the top of the mouth somehow folds over itself and over her head, so that everything that was inside her throat is now outside it - and I see two rows of sharply serrated teeth slide out of her skin until her entire head has become something very like the only weapon at a venus flytrap's disposal, the trap itself. I realise that the only reason I had to believe her high humanity was her besotted mother's constant repetition of a statistic. A statistic, I realise, means nothing. A mouth full of teeth biting into your face means everything. I've not got much human blood in me, but in pain and panic I feel it starting to drain, my human blood and my chlorophyll starting to separate, the one pooling out of me, the other being drawn up into those teeth as though they are hyperdermic needles. Then a shot rings out, and my last thought as I black out is that venus flytraps never hide to catch their prey - they just stay very very open, until you think it's all safe. And then it's all over in less than a second.

* * *

When I come to I'm strapped to an ambulance stretcher and feel weaker than I ever have in my whole life. I don't know where I am but can hear the hubbub of people all around me. I feel numb and toxified and barely able to move. That's when I realise that if I want to see anything, I'd probably better try to open my eyes.

The dark, rough-red face of Lieutenant Solo looms above me. I blink my eyes a couple of times and he swings into focus. I wonder how long he's been there.

"Don't try to move too much," he says. "You're safe. But you're on a rhesus drip. You'll be weak as a budling for a couple of days, copchild."

This not knowing is unbearable. "What happened?" I ask.

"The medics are taking traces of Juliette Perrez's body. She's not a flytrap as we know it, so the police are steering away from making any potentially dangerous official statements to the effect that Rosie Field's murderer was a venus flytrap - they don't want a hate crime backlash, after all. Who does? We don't know what Juliette Perrez was. She certainly wasn't human. Cops are interviewing her mother back at HQ, and it seems the mother knew something was wrong with Juliette from day one. She seems to be covering it up though. Nothing shows up on the lie detectors. When she states Juliette Perrez was nearly fully human, she clearly believes everything she's saying. She's clearly in the grip of major denial."

"Is Juliette dead?" I ask. "How is she dead? If she wasn't a flytrap, what was she?"

"We don't know. Flora Perrez swears that Juliette's father was another flytrap and lie detectors seem to be corroborating that, for what it's worth. The cops reckon Juliette Perrez was just a freak of nature."

"And you?"

"We're all freaks, Greensleeves. We just slap cop badges and labels on ourselves and call ourselves a functioning society, but we're all a mixed-up bag of genes that nature never asked for and never wanted, wouldn't you say? Juliette was just more of a freak than the rest of us. She was very alone."

"Tell me, Solo. I don't understand. Is she dead?"

"She's dead," he says, and I can hear the sadness in his voice. "Forensics say that when she changed she couldn't get a full grip on your face because she kept slipping off the full foliage of your hair, and cops came down to find you after you requisitioned the ceasing of the club's alarm - they pulled their guns on her just in time."

I look into Solo's eyes as best I can with my muzzy-headed confusion. I feel poisoned. I think she poisoned me. That's why I didn't struggle when her teeth bit deep. I don't know why she bit me, or Rosie Fields. Maybe she was hungry. I don't know anything anymore.

"You're forensics, Solo." I try to say it quietly, but my ears feel like they're filled with cotton wool and I can't tell if I'm whispering or shouting. "What was her last dream?"

He gives me a look. "I couldn't do that, Greensleeves. Don't go there. I could give you clues, because I knew there was something wrong with her, I knew she might be a killer - but I couldn't do that."

And that's when I admitted to myself, finally, why I'd seen a photo of Lieutenant Solo on the dressing room table of Juliette Perrez.

"I feel really tired, Solo. So tired. Can you just tell me - what's it like to be in love?"

He bends down and gently brushes my eyelids shut with his rough fingers. I feel the warm rasp of his kiss on my forehead, then on each eye.

"You're too young to know that yet, petalcop. Just know that we all have a case like this - the one that makes us grown, even if it's in a way we don't want. The case that follows us round every dark corner and in our dreams that we can't escape from. It makes us better cops. That's all."

I'm so tired, I just want to slip quietly away, but I can still feel my forehead and eyelids. They feel nice. Maybe nothing else does, but they feel nice.

"And better people?" I'm thinking of my Immobile dad, and if he'd be proud of me.

But Solo doesn't answer, and when I hear his voice again it's from a few paces off, and as it gets quieter I can tell he's walking away from me. I think he's singing. I've never heard him sing before.

"Greensleeves was my one delight - who but my lady Greensleeves."

About Magda Knight

Magda Knight is the founder and editor of Mookychick Online, *a feminist community for alternative girls and women, with a quarter of a million visitors per month. She has previously been published in the longstanding national UK comic* 2000AD, *and her work has appeared in the anthology* What Would Bill Hicks Say?

Justifications for Deception

by David R. Jones

That date tree has had its eyes on me. It has been eyeing me up and down like a piece of steak freshly grilled and drip-drip-dripping with inner juices simmering up and out, the tender and aromatic flesh sending plumes of smoke wafting like clouds in its direction. That date tree has a nose somewhere between its branches and it breathes in deeply as the wafting aroma of my juiciness passes it by. It inhales and thinks, "That's delicious and I want some." That date tree wants me. It wants me like I am a street-corner hooker.

"Let me be! *Hssssss*."

I shriek and hiss, and now I'm back to scavenging and eating. Why won't that date tree let me be? Look how its branches billow over to the left to whisper into the leaves of that nearby palm saying, "Look what we have here: a delicious feast for the eyes and our lust." Now the palm smacks its lips. Now it, too, has caught the scent of my simmering deliciousness.

I pretend that I don't see, but I do. I see it. I see it everyday and I shriek and flash obscene gestures. One time I sharpened the point of a stick with a broken shard of rock. I sharpened the point of the stick as keen as a scimitar's edge. I lofted my weapon and made a mock charge against that cluster of trees all eyeing me like a whore. I charged them with wild, maniacal abandon like I hadn't the least reservation about plunging them through their xyloid hearts. I only pretended though; I had no real intention of ever hurting them. I wanted my privacy.

I want my privacy now. A man shouldn't have to worry about such things like the denigrating stares of tropical trees suggesting lasciviousness toward my form. Perhaps if I had the chance to shower—I mean, a real shower, and not the clumsy dashing through saline waves running headlong toward the beach shores of my lonely island: that isn't really bathing, but more like making do with my circumstances. If I had the chance to shave my beard and cut my hair, rather than knotting it and pasting my hair in clumps flat against my head with grease from the gutted bellies of rotted fish that washed ashore, I might protest less. I might feel a bit more like that I deserved this kind of attention. But how they stare at me now is like they think they can take advantage of me without remonstrance.

Pretty or not, I would rather have my privacy for now. Something about fishing through rat dung for chunks of digestible food makes me feel less pretty. Maybe this is embarrassment that I feel. Or something of shame. I should know how to hunt. I wish I knew how to hunt. Then again, there isn't anything on this island for hunting, except maybe the rats, and the island doesn't have enough of those. If I killed one or two each day then I would have no more left to rely on and what could I do then? So I content myself and sort through their droppings. When I am fortunate enough to find three or four piles a day, I can scavenge a hearty meal. I am more or less a parasite.

The biggest regret I have about my paltry diet—bigger, even, than the denigration of eating crap and relying on rats for sustenance—is that I haven't the energy to make anything more of myself. That isn't to say that I could make much while stranded on a lonely tropical island all alone. I could have a bit of fruit from that date tree if only I wasn't so afraid of being raped. That date tree has had its eye on me. But if I could find the energy, I might find ways of fashioning a spear with a long strand of rope so that I could catch myself some live fish. I might even find a way to build a fire. I should have learned how to do these things. But I can't.

I gave up scrounging after discovering only a few seeds embedded in the pellets of feces. I need to let the rats alone for longer so they can eat in peace and store up heartier portions. Or maybe the rats have become too numerous and they each have less to eat. Maybe the rats have become too many and I should kill one or two a week, just to balance out the population so that the survivors have a chance to eat heartier potions to leave me tidbits. I should have learned how to kill rats. I wish I knew how to make traps.

I retreat to the far side of the island and sit myself under the last strip of shade where the beach ends and the undergrowth begins. I stretch my legs out across the bright, warm sand. But while I'm sitting there I can hear them whispering, the date and the palm, talking about me. So I look over my shoulder every once in a while and give them ugly glares. I try to focus on the cadence of the waves. I try to predict which waves will reach up to splash the heels of my feet.

I used to divide my time between different sides of the island. Then I gave it up and resigned myself to the tedium of one area. I resigned myself because the island, being so small and so remote, really only gave a single kind of perspective which didn't change no matter how hard you looked, no matter if you changed how you looked at it.

Since forever the island has amounted to little more than a slight knoll bulging from the ocean's belly button, although I can't say what ocean. Its breadth spans twenty giant, exaggerated steps across its diameter. A shrub on the side where the sun shines least tells me that the island once had more space but it all washed back into the sea as little grains of bleached sand. I don't credit the shrub for much though, and it makes me itch all over which probably means I should trust it less. The island has about ten trees, eight of which are palm trees that I don't mind. Of course I hate the other two: they two perverts, I call them, because they only ever stare at me with leering, suggestive glances.

On my side of the island—the side I use most often—I keep a calendar. The calendar keeps me sane. It keeps going forward, adding days at a time. If I didn't have the calendar, I might not know to expect it to happen—escaping the little island, death, or whatever else awaits me. I mark every day after waking and I check it before going to sleep to see how many days I have finished. I tell myself, "Hey, it's coming sooner now, whatever 'it' happens to be, it's coming sooner."

My calendar changes, too, and the changing makes a difference—an awfully big difference. Nothing else changes on the island. Even my beard and hair stopped growing longer. My calendar changes, though, and the changing brings about some relief. I look at the calendar, starting from the top left, reading along toward the right.

I started with dots that later became more box-shaped and now more intentionally square. I ran out of room after a few months—not that I ran out of room on the island, only that I had to keep the calendar within certain bounds because certain factors might damage it, like rising tidal waves or the rats, and so on. Instead of growing my calendar larger, I went back to the beginning and formed a circle of smaller dots around the squares. I liked making the dots: they didn't require much besides poking your finger down straight through the sand until the sand covered half of my fingernail.

While I'm reading, a tiny crab tries to burrow into my two thousand, seven hundred and ninety second day.

"Ah!" I shriek.

But tiny crabs don't hear very well and this one doesn't seem to care at all that I yelled at it. I should have studied marine biology. I wish I had studied biology. I find a light pebble washed up just behind me, maybe a step away. So I pick it up and fling it at the tiny crab which only prompts the crab to dash deep down into my calendar, rather than chasing him away as I had hoped to do. As it crawls deep down, it leers at me, threatens me.

"I'll make mush of your calendar. I'll burrow a giant expanse beneath your calendar so that all of your hard work and your sanity collapse."

The tiny crab disappears into my two thousand, seven hundred and ninety second day laughing at me and the peels of its laughter echo against the tunnel walls as it descends deeper and deeper.

I approach close and crouch down so that I can better jam pinches of sand down into the burrow after the tiny crab. My attempt to suffocate it. Bastard. I expend too much energy and emotion, and I grow dizzy and faint. I collapse onto the sand. I am about to lose consciousness and sleep. I don't mind because the sun has already started dropping and will disappear soon so there won't be anything left to do for the day, but my feet are too close to the water and when tide rises, they will get wet and stay cold all night. I wish I had the energy to move. I wish I could at least move my feet.

Seconds from my eyelids shut, my gaze catches the edge of my calendar. I see a spot that seems smoothed over clean. Maybe it's that one of my days is erased. Did I erase a day? I wouldn't do that, but I can't remember for sure. I do crazy things some times, like the time I gave up and I jumped into the ocean and began swimming for the point on the horizon furthest from this shithole island. I swam past the breaking waves and past the cresting waves and past the climbing waves. I had better muscle build then because I hadn't lived so long from picking through feces for seeds. I had better muscle build but I still wore down quickly. I fainted. I know I did. I know my arms stopped reaching and my legs stopped kicking and my head stopped tilting upward for gulps of air. But I didn't die. I woke up with feces-reeking seeds stuck to my lips, lying with my back on the bright, hot sand, staring upward into the vast, blue sky and blinding aura of sunlight. I did crazy. Crazy did me a higher hand and beat me.

My dimming gaze still ponders the smooth spot on my calendar. Did I make a mark for today? I extend my tongue and reach to the smooth spot. My body writhes from the discomfort of the strain and the summons of energy reserves that no longer exist. Tongue touches sand, tastes the gritty, and presses a slight indent. The tongue comes back inside my mouth and I taste sand, but I'm too exhausted to spit it out and my eyes go dark anyway as I slide into sleep.

I dream an image of a pale, metallic desk separating a cleaner, more civilized version of me from a man on the opposite side dressed as some sort of doctor, holding a clipboard. He wears wire-rimmed glasses; wild, disheveled hair; and professor-like clothes. To one side of the desk, along the wall, I can see a room through a darkened glass. The doctor-looking man doesn't tell me but I bet that the adjacent room that I can see through the darkened glass serves for observation and people in the adjacent room can't see back through the darkened glass into the room where we are sitting.

Man: The point is to answer as honestly as possible.

Me, the cleaner version: Oh sure, I understand. And you'll tell me if there's a better way to answer?

Man: (*Sigh*) I've told you already a time or two that there isn't a right or wrong response. But I need you to answer me instead of probing me for more questions.

Me: I'm sorry. Does that mean I can't participate?

Man: You're doing it again.

Me: It's just that I need the money. Tell me again how much I'm earning.

Man: You can clarify the details of the experiment with the assistant as you leave today.

Me: Does that mean I can't participate—because I have to leave?

Man: (*While removing glasses and pinching the bridge of nose*) Really, this is getting to be too much. As you learned earlier, today's visit serves the purpose of completing some associated paperwork and clarifying some information in preparation of your return tomorrow when the experiment will officially begin.

Me: (*Fingertips anxiously rubbing against each other*) And the money?

Man: (*Replacing glasses to face, turning slightly in chair to cross legs without striking the desk*) You'll discuss those particulars as you leave this interview.

Me: Okay. I'm sorry. I'll try to focus now.

Man: (*Picking clipboard up from lap and running a finger down along the face of it until he finds the entry he seeks*) Do you have any trade experience? Any technical expertise? Mechanical employment? Etc.?

Me: Would that help? I can read up on it, maybe figure some stuff out.

Man: It would help if you answered the question honestly and changed nothing about your situation between now and tomorrow.

Me: (*Starting to speak and stopping and thinking like I'm trying to figure out the consequences for my response before I give it and then finally giving up because I haven't a clue how the doctor man will judge me*) No.

Man: No to which part?

Me: All of it. I never had any kind of training or job where I had to know how to fix things. My dad couldn't even do half of those things— he died young, you know—and I couldn't learn from him while he was alive 'cause he always explained things like, "This here thingamajigger holds all of the water so you got to turn the knobby-knob righty-tighty before you loosen the thingy here." So is it really my fault I didn't learn how to fix a simple leak? Could you have learned like that?

Man: I suppose not.

Me: I'm sorry. That sounded rude, huh?

Man: I'm not here to pass condemnation or judgment. Let's continue. Have you ever participated in outdoor excursions similar to or exactly like hunting, fishing, hiking, climbing, swimming, farming, trapping, camping, etc.?

Me: Um, no.

Man: (*scribbles something on his clipboard*)

Me: Will I have to for the experiment?

Man: I can't give you details yet about the experiment, just consider these hypothetical questions.

Me: Hypothetical of what?

Man: Uh, let's continue. Shall we? In the event of an emergency, whom should we contact?

Me: What kind of emergency?

Man: Again, the question is hypo—er, uh, procedural. I ask the question just for the sake of satisfying a generic procedure that's administered to everyone.

Me: So I won't get hurt?

Man: Um.

Me: That's good to know. You can contact my wife—no, not my wife. Contact my brother and he can decide who else to contact. He has a wife so he understands what kind of information worries a wife and what things a wife absolutely must know.

Man: Do you have any objections or specifications for receiving therapeutic services following your participation?

Me: Another hypothetical question?

Man: Well, not really. We do expect you to attend some debriefing sessions after the experiment.

Me: Why?

Man: Just to make sure that you feel alright.

Me: I feel alright. I feel fine.

Man: Well, we are more concerned about your status after the experiment.

Me: Will I feel sad?

Man: Very improbable. Probably nothing bad will come of your participation and the ensuing therapeutic experience will ensure that.

Me: Oh. What is the experiment for?

Man: Um.

Me: I mean, like, what are you studying?

Man: Let's say that it has something to do with how perceptions of time impact humans.

Me: That sounds important.

Man: We think so.

I have this dream when I'm sleeping and sometimes when I'm waiting with my eyes wide open about two men, one of whom looks a lot like the way I think I might look, talking across a cold, metal desk. Maybe I had a life like that before I arrived here. Maybe I aspire to a life like that once I get off of this island. Maybe I'm crazy. I should have studied psychology. I wish I understood psychology.

This time I have the dream while I'm sleeping. I realize I'm sleeping because the feeling of wet and cold turns on gradually even though I can tell the wet and cold have been there for a while. When I dream awake these things hit me just as suddenly as they happen. Sometimes it takes these things a moment or so to register on my senses, but I still have the reaction of startling because I sensed it all at once.

My senses turn on one by one so that I can smell the salt and hear the ground quaking as the waves pound the shore and I can feel the side of my face pressed flat-squished. My sight returns last. I possess this surreal awareness of the world burning through my eyelids and I think that it might be beautiful until I actually open my eyes.

I am lying on the sand beside my calendar. The waves lap at my ankles but I don't mind: they will recede back into low tide and the heat will draw the blood back into my feet. My strength hasn't returned yet, only my mental capacity, supposing I have any remaining. I can focus my senses, though, and I do. I see the early-morning pale blue of the sky above me. I hear the steady cadence of waves advancing, crashing, retreating, and returning. My mouth tastes like rot. I feel the sun rays that streak from the distant horizon as they skip across my back. I feel the grains of sand exfoliating the downturned half of my face. I also feel sand grains scratching against folds of skin covered by my tattered, besmirched, and reeking shreds of clothing.

My eyes steadily focus. At first they study only the abstract forms of things. They tune to the color and shades and hues. Then they draw out the details. I look all about me as I continue laying on my side. I see a spot on my calendar that seems smoothed over clean. Maybe it's that one of my days is erased. Did I erase a day? I don't think I did that, but I do crazy things some times. I move my hands up and lazily impress my fingertip to indicate another day.

About David R. Jones

Davey studied literature and psychology at the University of Michigan and later received a Master's in counseling from California State University. He lives in Fresno, California with his wife and an overabundance of animals that the couple often mistakes for children.

Frame Zero

by C. Stuart Hardwick

C. Stuart Hardwick's short story, *Frame Zero,* was chosen as the winner of the 2011 fourth quarter round. As fate would have it, Mr. Hardwick has opted out of our anthology in the hopes that *Frame Zero* might be worth more to him in the long run. Honestly, we can't blame him. It was certainly a winning story. For more from Hardwick, visit http://cstuarthardwick.wordpress.com/

About C. Stuart Hardwick

When C. Stuart Hardwick was told he had a knack for writing compelling stories, he did what seemed logical: went into computers instead. The stories, however, wouldn't let him alone. He had spent his childhood roaming the desolate badlands and wind-blown ghost towns of South Dakota, where the rich tapestry of geologic time, the adventures of the Wild West, and the promise of the space age all intersected to inflame his imagination.

A science-fair robot and a few years in consumer software led to a career distinguished by dedication to communications and design. Today, he's a systems architect and an award winning author--two sides of the same coin, since prose is the user interface of literature. He still finds inspiration in life's crossroads and connections, and in the irrepressible human spirit that drives us to dream of worlds beyond our own.